U0097853

TOEIC

練習測驗（2）

LISTENING TEST

In the Listening test, you will be asked to demonstrate how well you understand spoken English. The entire Listening test will last approximately 45 minutes. There are four parts, and directions are given for each part. You must mark your answers on the separate answer sheet. Do not write your answers in your test book.

PART 1

Directions: For each question in this part, you will hear four statements about a picture in your test book. When you hear the statements, you must select the one statement that best describes what you see in the picture. Then find the number of the question on your answer sheet and mark your answer. The statements will not be printed in your test book and will be spoken only one time.

Statement (C), "They're sitting at a table," is the best description of the picture, so you should select answer (C) and mark it on your answer sheet.

1.

2.

GO ON TO THE NEXT PAGE.

3.

4.

5.

6.

GO ON TO THE NEXT PAGE

PART 2

Directions: You will hear a question or statement and three responses spoken in English. They will not be printed in your test book and will be spoken only one time. Select the best response to the question or statement and mark the letter (A), (B), or (C) on your answer sheet.

7. Mark your answer on your answer sheet.

8. Mark your answer on your answer sheet.

9. Mark your answer on your answer sheet.

10. Mark your answer on your answer sheet.

11. Mark your answer on your answer sheet.

12. Mark your answer on your answer sheet.

13. Mark your answer on your answer sheet.

14. Mark your answer on your answer sheet.

15. Mark your answer on your answer sheet.

16. Mark your answer on your answer sheet.

17. Mark your answer on your answer sheet.

18. Mark your answer on your answer sheet.

19. Mark your answer on your answer sheet.

20. Mark your answer on your answer sheet.

21. Mark your answer on your answer sheet.

22. Mark your answer on your answer sheet.

23. Mark your answer on your answer sheet.

24. Mark your answer on your answer sheet.

25. Mark your answer on your answer sheet.

26. Mark your answer on your answer sheet.

27. Mark your answer on your answer sheet.

28. Mark your answer on your answer sheet.

29. Mark your answer on your answer sheet.

30. Mark your answer on your answer sheet.

31. Mark your answer on your answer sheet.

Directions: You will hear some conversations between two people. You will be asked to answer three questions about what the speakers say in each conversation. Select the best response to each question and mark the letter (A), (B), (C), or (D) on your answer sheet. The conversation will not be printed in your test book and will be spoken only one time.

32. Where, most likely, do the speakers work?
    (A) At a post office.
    (B) At a catering business.
    (C) At a jewelry store.
    (D) At a flower shop.

33. What problem does the man mention?
    (A) A delivery did not arrive.
    (B) A customer made a complaint.
    (C) An employee was late.
    (D) A dinner was canceled.

34. What does the woman mean when she says, "Are you kidding?"?
    (A) She strongly disagrees.
    (B) She would like an explanation.
    (C) She feels disappointed.
    (D) She is pleasantly surprised.

35. What are the speakers mainly discussing?
    (A) A project proposal.
    (B) A work schedule.
    (C) A job opening.
    (D) An office layout.

36. What problem does the woman mention?
    (A) She has a long commute.
    (B) Renovations are very expensive.
    (C) She missed a deadline.
    (D) A work space is too quiet.

37. What will the woman probably do next week?
    (A) Transfer to another department.
    (B) Work longer hours.
    (C) Switch cubicles with another employee.
    (D) Listen to the radio while she works.

38. Why is the woman calling?
    (A) A membership has expired.
    (B) A lost item was found.
    (C) An order has arrived.
    (D) A video is overdue.

39. What does the man ask about?
    (A) Applying for a job.
    (B) Renewing an item.
    (C) Taking a class.
    (D) Researching a topic.

40. What does the man plan to do this afternoon?
    (A) Give a presentation.
    (B) Pay the fine.
    (C) Take the day off.
    (D) Purchase a book.

41. What did woman do yesterday?
    (A) She updated a manual.
    (B) She inspected a facility.
    (C) She returned from a trip.
    (D) She taught a class.

42. What does the man ask the woman to do?
    (A) Repeat a tutorial.
    (B) Speak with her supervisor.
    (C) Send notes from a trade show.
    (D) Evaluate some software.

43. What problem does the woman mention?
    (A) She is missing a document.
    (B) She has not received a payment.
    (C) She is not available next week.
    (D) She does not know a password.

GO ON TO THE NEXT PAGE.

44. What does the man ask about the apartment?
    (A) How many rooms it has.
    (B) How much it costs.
    (C) When it is available.
    (D) Where it is.

45. What is unique about the apartment?
    (A) Its storage space.
    (B) Its architectural details.
    (C) Its scenic view.
    (D) Its upgraded appliances.

46. What does the man mean when he says, "For sure"?
    (A) He would like to see the apartment.
    (B) He would like to sign the contract.
    (C) He agrees to pay the deposit.
    (D) He knows where the apartment is located.

47. What are the speakers mainly discussing?
    (A) The announcement of a new manager.
    (B) The introduction of a special service.
    (C) Plans for increasing business.
    (D) Procedures for a departmental process.

48. What will happen in July?
    (A) Television advertisements will be launched.
    (B) Client testimonials will be posted online.
    (C) A new Internet bank will be established.
    (D) An advertising agency will be hired.

49. What does Woman A say will appeal to customers?
    (A) Foreign currency exchange.
    (B) Extended business hours.
    (C) Home loans.
    (D) Online banking.

International Trade Conference
Wilton Hotel, Baltimore, MD
Saturday, November 19

10:00 A.M.-12:00 P.M.
"Transportation modes and how they can affect your supply chain"
Sponsored by DuPree Logistics –
Drew Flint, Senior Partner
Meeting Room 101

12:00 Noon-1:15 P.M.
Lunch
Wilton Hotel – Wolfgang Puck's Spoon

1:30 P.M.-3:00 P.M.
"Asia: A strategic approach to your Asian marketing plan"
Sponsored by Blackbox Associates –
Karen Hatrick, Chief Operating Officer
Meeting Room 102

3:15 P.M. -4:00 P.M.
Closing Ceremony
Wilton Ballroom

50. Who is the man?
    (A) An expert in international trade.
    (B) An event coordinator.
    (C) A trade representative.
    (D) An owner of an agency.

51. What has the woman agreed to do?
    (A) Lead a conference session.
    (B) Conduct an interview.
    (C) Schedule an appointment.
    (D) Accept a new position.

52. Look at the graphic. Who does the woman work for?
    (A) DuPree Logistics.
    (B) The Wilton Hotel.
    (C) Wolfgang Puck's Spoon.
    (D) Blackbox Associates.

PEERLESS WEB SERVICES

Custom Design and Support

20% OFF

Professional Web design services specializing in corporate and small business accounts

Visit our website to preview our work at **www.peerlessweb.com** *Mention this ad and receive 20% off your custom design package*

Tel: 712-333-0909
Ad Code: PWS-009

PWS

53. What kind of business does the woman run?
(A) A marketing firm.
(B) A catering service.
(C) An employment agency.
(D) A web design company.

54. What does the man offer to do?
(A) Help interview job candidates.
(B) Review a budget.
(C) Recommend the woman's business.
(D) Write a resume.

55. Look at the graphic. How can potential customers receive a discount?
(A) By mentioning the ad.
(B) By presenting a coupon.
(C) By signing up for a newsletter.
(D By placing an order before the end of the month.

56. Why is the woman calling?
(A) To ask about a missing item.
(B) To discuss a seating arrangement.
(C) To complain about a bill.
(D) To cancel a reservation.

57. What does the man tell the woman to bring?
(A) A bill.
(B) A completed form.
(C) A guest list.
(D) A credit card.

58. Where will the woman most likely go this afternoon?
(A) To a police station.
(B) To a client's office.
(C) To a restaurant.
(D) To a bank.

CompCore Product List COMPUTER PACKAGES (INCLUDES MONITOR)	
Screen Size	**Price**
SILVER Antel PC 866GHz processor 15" LCD monitor	$799
GOLD Antel PC 866GHZ processor 18" LCD monitor	$899
PLATINUM Antel PC 1.4GHz processor 18" LED monitor	$1099
PLATINUM PLUS Antel PC 1.4GHz processor 21" LCD monitor	$1199
DIAMOND Antel PC 2.2 GHZ processor 21" LED	$1299
DIAMOND PLUS Antel PC 2.2GHz processor 23" LCD	$1399

59. What does the woman ask the man to do?
(A) Write a proposal.
(B) Contact a job candidate.
(C) Order some equipment.
(D) Find a new vendor.

60. What problem does the man mention?
(A) A computer model has been discontinued.
(B) A departmental budget has been reduced.
(C) A designer has left the company.
(D) A supplier has increased its prices.

61. Look at the graphic. What size screen will the man order?
(A) 15 inches.
(B) 18 inches.
(C) 21 inches.
(D) 23 inches.

GO ON TO THE NEXT PAGE

If you are currently a medical student looking to make some extra money this summer, our leading medical research firm has openings for paid interns

Paid Medical Internship

Must have a GPA of 3.0 or higher and be currently enrolled in an accredited Pre-Med program

Facility is located in Foster City Transportation allowance provided for commuters

Tel: 413-356-7799

BioSearch Ltd.

Dr. Philip Baines

62. What does the man want to do?
(A) Hire an intern.
(B) Write a paper.
(C) Find a new job.
(D) Conduct some research.

63. Why did the woman contact the university?
(A) To sign up for a course.
(B) To submit a research proposal.
(C) To borrow the equipment.
(D) To find qualified job applicants.

64. Look at the graphic. What is required for the internship?
(A) A reliable vehicle.
(B) A master's degree.
(C) A grade point average of 3.0 or above.
(D) A valid medical license.

65. Why is the woman calling?
(A) To find out about a sale.
(B) To sign up for membership.
(C) To arrange a lecture.
(D) To ask about a schedule.

66. What does the man recommend?
(A) Checking an exhibit floor plan.
(B) Arriving early to an event.
(C) Signing up for a membership program.
(D) Buying tickets online.

67. What is the aquarium going to offer during the summer?
(A) Child care.
(B) Interpretive dance lessons.
(C) Free admission.
(D) Special tours.

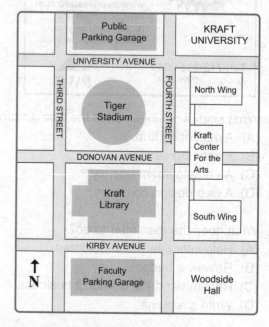

68. What does the woman request?
(A) A different rental car.
(B) A street map.
(C) A bus schedule.
(D) A temporary parking permit.

69. What does the man suggest?
(A) Paying with a credit card.
(B) Using an alternative parking area.
(C) Selecting a smaller vehicle.
(D) Rescheduling a lecture.

70. Look at the graphic. How far is Ms. McAllister from the Public Parking Garage right now?
(A) One block.
(B) Two blocks.
(C) Three blocks.
(D) Four blocks.

Directions: You will hear some talks given by a single speaker. You will be asked to answer three questions about what the speaker says in each talk. Select the best response to each question and mark the letter (A), (B), (C), or (D) on your answer sheet. The talks will not be printed in your test book and will be spoken only one time.

71. What is the purpose of the speaker's visit?
  (A) To present research findings.
  (B) To promote a new product.
  (C) To improve worker efficiency.
  (D) To explain a corporate procedure.

72. According to the speaker, what are the listeners planning to do next year?
  (A) Open an overseas office.
  (B) Design a building.
  (C) Restructure a department.
  (D) Host a trade show.

73. What will the speaker most likely do next?
  (A) Answer some questions.
  (B) Distribute some documents.
  (C) Introduce a guest.
  (D) Complete an installation.

74. What product is being discussed?
  (A) An energy drink.
  (B) A vitamin supplement.
  (C) A breakfast cereal.
  (D) A nutrition bar.

75. What concern does the caller mention?
  (A) A product name is not repeated.
  (B) A focus group did not like a flavor.
  (C) A song is too long.
  (D) A package is difficult to open.

76. What does the speaker request that the listener do?
  (A) Send additional samples.
  (B) Come to the company headquarters.
  (C) Suggest another name.
  (D) Record a song again.

77. What is the broadcast mainly about?
  (A) An international award.
  (B) A scientific discovery.
  (C) A sports competition.
  (D) An upcoming conference.

78. According to the speaker, what can listeners do on a Web site?
  (A) Read an article.
  (B) Enter a contest.
  (C) Check program listings.
  (D) View photographs.

79. Who is Dr. Gabriel Dyson?
  (A) A tour guide.
  (B) An astronomer.
  (C) A journalist.
  (D) A nutritionist.

80. Who is the intended audience of the talk?
  (A) Computer repair technicians.
  (B) Customer service representatives.
  (C) Financial advisers.
  (D) Legal assistants.

81. How will listeners be trained?
  (A) By watching online videos.
  (B) By attending a series of workshops.
  (C) By reading an employee handbook.
  (D) By working with experienced employees.

82. What does the speaker say will happen at the end of the week?
  (A) New employees will be evaluated.
  (B) Participants will attend a banquet.
  (C) Policies will be updated.
  (D) Schedules will be posted.

GO ON TO THE NEXT PAGE

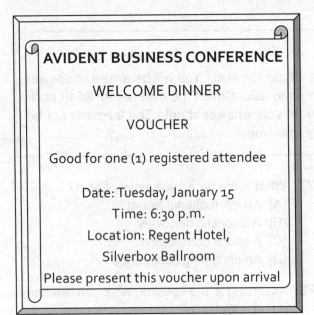

AVIDENT BUSINESS CONFERENCE

WELCOME DINNER

VOUCHER

Good for one (1) registered attendee

Date: Tuesday, January 15
Time: 6:30 p.m.
Location: Regent Hotel,
Silverbox Ballroom
Please present this voucher upon arrival

83. Who most likely are the listeners?
(A) Concert performers.
(B) Technical support staff.
(C) Conference attendees.
(D) Restaurant servers.

84. What problem does the speaker mention?
(A) A room has not been reserved.
(B) Some tickets were not distributed.
(C) A speaker is unavailable.
(D) A microphone is not working.

85. Look at the graphic. Where will the dinner be held?
(A) In a cafeteria.
(B) In a conference room.
(C) In a hotel ballroom.
(D) In a casual restaurant.

86. Where does the speaker most likely work?
(A) At a local airport.
(B) At a fitness magazine.
(C) At a martial arts school.
(D) At a travel agency.

87. Why does the speaker apologize?
(A) He has missed a publication deadline.
(B) He has misplaced a set of keys.
(C) He is unable to attend a meeting.
(D) He cannot access a computer network.

88. What is the speaker pleased about?
(A) The features of a new software system.
(B) The changes to an advertising budget.
(C) The number of people at an event.
(D) The performance of some team members.

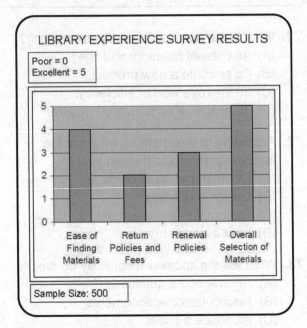

LIBRARY EXPERIENCE SURVEY RESULTS

Poor = 0
Excellent = 5

Sample Size: 500

89. Look at the graphic. What are library patrons most pleased with?
(A) Renewal policies.
(B) Overall selection.
(C) Ease of access to materials.
(D) Wait times at the information desk.

90. What does the woman mean when she says, "On a positive note"?
(A) She will answer some questions.
(B) She wants the listeners to take notes.
(C) She will introduce a different subject.
(D) She has more bad news for the listeners.

91. What does the speaker say about the library's information desk?
(A) It is understaffed.
(B) It is being repaired.
(C) It has recently been relocated.
(D) It will get a faster Internet connection.

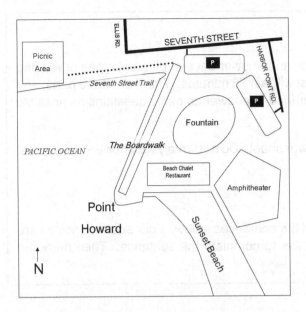

Picnic Area

SEVENTH STREET

ELLIS RD.

Seventh Street Trail

HARBOR POINT RD.

P

P

Fountain

The Boardwalk

PACIFIC OCEAN

Beach Chalet Restaurant

Amphitheater

Point

Howard

Sunset Beach

N

92. Look at the graphic. Where will the listeners be unable to go on Sunday?
(A) The Boardwalk.
(B) The Picnic Area.
(C) Harbor Point Road.
(D) Sunset Beach.

93. What is said about the beach?
(A) It will be under construction.
(B) It will cost money to cross.
(C) It will be closed to traffic.
(D) It will provide a good view.

94. What is scheduled for Sunday?
(A) A sporting event.
(B) A city celebration.
(C) A local election.
(D) A walking tour.

95. What does the speaker remind listeners of?
(A) A transfer procedure.
(B) Luggage restrictions.
(C) A frequent-flier program.
(D) In-flight meal options.

96. What was the cause of the delay?
(A) An airplane was undergoing a routine check.
(B) There was heavier air traffic than expected.
(C) An airplane needed more fuel.
(D) There was bad weather in the area.

97. What does the speaker request that listeners do?
(A) Move to a different waiting area.
(B) Accept new seat assignments.
(C) Claim their belongings.
(D) Have their boarding passes ready.

98. What type of merchandise is being advertised?
(A) Hardware.
(B) Small electronics.
(C) Packing materials.
(D) Clothing.

99. How can customers receive a discount on Monday?
(A) By purchasing larger boxes.
(B) By referring to an advertisement.
(C) By presenting a coupon.
(D) By opening a line of credit.

100. According to the speaker, what additional service does the store provide?
(A) Orders are shipped free of charge.
(B) Representatives are available 24 hours a day.
(C) Customers can preorder merchandise.
(D) Gift wrapping is complimentary with every purchase.

This is the end of the Listening test. Turn to Part 5 in your test book.

GO ON TO THE NEXT PAGE.

READING TEST

In the Reading test, you will read a variety of texts and answer several different types of reading comprehension questions. The entire Reading test will last 75 minutes. There are three parts, and directions are given for each part. You are encouraged to answer as many questions as possible within the time allowed.

You must mark your answers on the separate answer sheet. Do not write your answers in your test book.

PART 5

Directions: A word or phrase is missing in each of the sentences below. Four answer choices are given below each sentence. Select the best answer to complete the sentence. Then mark the letter (A), (B), (C), or (D) on your answer sheet.

101. All first-year lab technicians and research assistants at Triton Biomedical Inc. must have ------- a general orientation program.
(A) attending
(B) attends
(C) attend
(D) attended

102. Bloomfield Capital Equity provides financial advice ------- manages customer investment portfolios with a value of $500,000 or more.
(A) either
(B) for
(C) until
(D) and

103. Tom's Texas BBQ is the most ------- addition to the Allied Group's roster of fast-food restaurants in the Houston area.
(A) recent
(B) lately
(C) last
(D) former

104. Generally speaking, most vendors will generate an invoice ------- their customers place a new order.
(A) since
(B) when
(C) even
(D) above

105. The library's offices are equipped with ------- doors that open when their motion sensors are triggered.
(A) bright
(B) irregular
(C) automatic
(D) frequent

106. The conference featured a discussion panel focused on staying ------- in the volatile Asian and European markets.
(A) competitive
(B) competitively
(C) competed
(D) competition

107. In the fourth quarter alone, Ripcurl Shoe Company slashed ------- 10,000 jobs from its overseas workforce.
(A) approximation
(B) approximate
(C) approximated
(D) approximately

108. Employees of Mellon Textile Industries are ------- prohibited from smoking anywhere on company property.
(A) heavily
(B) awkwardly
(C) strictly
(D) tensely

14

109. Many recent college graduates will spend months sending out resumes before finding ------- first professional job.
(A) them
(B) theirs
(C) them
(D) their

110. Initial results appear to indicate a win for the incumbent, but ------- the every vote is counted, it's still anyone's race.
(A) despite
(B) until
(C) yet
(D) still

111. The marketing team's ongoing ------- to improve brand recognition only recently began to pay off.
(A) conclusion
(B) attempt
(C) industry
(D) container

112. Upon his arrival, Mr. Ellis was ------- informed that his hotel reservation had been cancelled by an unknown party.
(A) mistake
(B) mistook
(C) mistakenly
(D) mistaken

113. Every branch of Green Valley Bank will now be open on Saturdays, ------- the main office on Kenmore Street.
(A) over
(B) considering
(C) than
(D) except

114. In times of financial turmoil, wise investors will seek to sell assets perceived as ------- and instead purchase safer commodities.
(A) risky
(B) concentrated
(C) decreased
(D) worthy

115. The majority of trendy restaurants and cafes are located in the southwest ------- of the city known as the Panhandle.
(A) area
(B) distance
(C) amount
(D) plan

116. Ever since he joined the firm, Joe Pollack ------- to be the leading defense attorney at Davis, Grubbs and Leith.
(A) aspiring
(B) has aspired
(C) aspire
(D) is aspiring

117. The training session is open to ------- who needs to get more familiar with the new software program.
(A) whichever
(B) other
(C) anyone
(D) themselves

118. Although many spectators were loud and unruly, the director ------- answered every question raised at the board meeting.
(A) instantaneously
(B) patiently
(C) simultaneously
(D) potentially

119. By working around the clock in three shifts, the automaker is able to ------- 50 full-sized vehicles per day.
(A) argue
(C) carry
(B) solve
(D) assemble

120. At the end of every project, Crestline Construction donates all leftover materials ------- local charitable organizations.
(A) of
(B) to
(C) by
(D) on

GO ON TO THE NEXT PAGE.

121. Since its ------- over 40 years ago,
Peerless Fabrication Inc. has
manufactured the best food service
equipment available.
(A) establish
(B) established
(C) establishment
(D) establishments

122. Many of the ------- flights to international
and domestic destinations can be
purchased from online clearing houses,
such as SkyBargains.com.
(A) cheapen
(B) cheapness
(C) cheapest
(D) cheaply

123. In acknowledgement of the city's -------
population, officials have allocated
millions of dollars to upgrade the city's
infrastructure.
(A) grew
(B) growth
(C) grow
(D) growing

124. Commuters are advised to plan on longer
travel times, since ------- people are
expected to attend the week-long festival.
(A) any
(B) many
(C) much
(D) every

125. The investigator's report concluded that
the accident would have been ------- had
the company followed its own safety
guidelines.
(A) preventing
(B) prevention
(C) prevent
(D) preventable

126. Rather than delegate the complicated
surgery to another resident, Dr. Michelle
Cooper opted to perform the procedure
-------.
(A) herself
(B) she
(C) hers
(D) her

127. To create a tropical atmosphere, the
landscape ------- recommended that palm
trees be planted on the property.
(A) to design
(B designing
(C) designed
(D) designer

128. According to a statement ------- by a
company spokesperson, Glover Oil will
appeal the verdict handed down by the
appellate court.
(A) issuing
(B) to issue
(C) was issued
(D) issued

129. ------- the most recent financial reports are
accurate, the company may still be forced
to declare bankruptcy before the end of
the year.
(A) Rather than
(B) According to
(C) Provided that
(D) Even if

130. Requests for vacation time should be
------- to the human resources department
at least two weeks in advance.
(A) selected
(B) assumed
(C) submitted
(D) needed

PART 6

Directions: Read the texts that follow. A word or phrase is missing in some of the sentences. Four answer choices are given below each of the sentences. Select the best answer to complete the text. Then mark the letter (A), (B), (C), or (D) on your answer sheet.

Questions 131-134 refer to the following advertisement.

PERSONNEL MANAGER WANTED

Quincy Marks Limited, an engineering firm located in Wilmington, Delaware, is looking for a manager to oversee its busy personnel department.

To be -------, candidates must have at least five years of managerial
    131.
experience.

The main ------- of the position will be recruiting new employees
    132.
with international business experience.

-------. These include the ------- of pay scales and benefits as well as
133.   **134.**
bonuses and other incentives. To download an application, visit
http://www.qml.com/careers

---

131. (A) licensed
    (B) considered
    (C) credited
    (D) motivated

132. (A) focal
    (B) focused
    (C) focus
    (D) focusing

133. (A) The interns will be compensated on a sliding scale, depending upon the amount of time served
    (B) The engineers will oversee all long-term projects and answer to department supervisors
    (C) The doctor will prescribe the appropriate medication for your condition
    (D) The manager will also be required to make decisions regarding financial compensation

134. (A) approval
    (B) conclusion
    (C) role
    (D) dedication

GO ON TO THE NEXT PAGE.

Questions 135-138 refer the following advertisement.

Serving Laurel Canyon for over 20 years

Sinclair & Sons

PROFESSIONAL LANDSCAPING

PROFESSIONAL
LANDSCAPING

765 Shaw Boulevard
Laurel Canyon, CA 90022

Phone: 418-222-0099
Fax: 418-222-0098
E-mail: sands@sinclair.com

Sinclair & Sons has been providing responsible
and professional landscape ------- services in
135.
Laurel Canyon for over 20 years.

Based on the principles of hard work and attention,
our certified landscapers ------- — everything from
136.
routine work, such as lawn mowing, pruning, and
gutter cleaning to major landscape installations,
including tree planting, debris removal, and garden
design.

We service all types of properties, commercial
and residential landscapes ------- .
137.

---------- .
138.

Another Green World

---

135. (A) sales
(B) maintenance
(C) manufacturing
(D) rental

136. (A) perform
(B) fasten
(C) construct
(D) transport

137. (A) similar
(B) each
(C) alike
(D) only

138. (A) To view the property, please reply to this email
(B) To schedule an estimate, please call us at
(418) 222-0099
(C) To speak with a customer service
representative, press 1
(D) To leave a message, wait for the tone

Grover-Morton Real Estate
19900 Atlantic Parkway
Miami Beach, FL 52228

April 5

Ms. Gina Guttas
909 Palm Dale Boulevard
Edgewater, FL 52598

Dear Ms. Guttas,

David Simpson indicated to me that you had gotten in touch with him about possibly relocating to Daytona Beach. ------- also mentioned that you have some special
139.
requirements when it comes to finding rehearsal space.

I have helped other musicians in similar situations, so I know how challenging it can be when one is ------- a suitable place to practice and perform.
140.

Fortunately, a new listing just appeared for a very spacious warehouse, which, as you can see in enclosed photographs, has ample room to construct your sound stage. ------- enough to meet your needs.
141.

We could then discuss the details and arrange for you to visit the property if you choose. I look forward to hearing ------- you. My phone number is 414-933-7734.
142.

Sincerely,
Wesley Grover

139. (A) They
    (B) We
    (C) It
    (D) He

140. (A) cleaning
    (B) renovating
    (C) selling
    (D) seeking

141. (A) Please let me know if you think this sweater would be warm
    (B) Please let me know if you think this property would be large
    (C) Please let me know if you think this office would be quiet
    (D) Please let me know if you think this station would be close

142. (A) with
    (B) by
    (C) from
    (D) at

GO ON TO THE NEXT PAGE.

Questions 143-146 refer to the following directions.

Crystal Paradise Resort: Getting here from Puerto Princesa by taxi or bus

From Puerto Princesa's main taxi depot, travel 23 kilometers south on Palawan Coastal Highway 1. You'll see our sign next to the guard house at the entrance to a banana plantation on the right side of the highway. The path leading to the resort is on the right side of the road, directly ------- the entrance to the banana plantation.
143.

From Puerto Princesa's central bus station, take any bus traveling toward Narra, and ask the driver to let ------- off at the Aborlan bus station.
144.

The resort is 2.9 kilometers south of the bus station.

For more information about -------, please visit our Web site,
145.

www.crystalparadise.com.

-------.
146.

---

143. (A) up
(B) across from
(C) along with
(D) between

144. (A) you
(B) yourselves
(C) your
(D) yours

145. (A) room rates
(B) lodging
(C) guided tours
(D) transportation

146. (A) The restaurant features nightly dinner specials
(B) The island features white sand beaches and abundant wildlife
(C) The tour features whale-watching and deep-sea fishing
(D) The home page features links to a road map and local traffic alerts

PART 7

Directions: In this part you will read a selection of texts, such as magazine and newspaper articles, e-mails, and instant messages. Each text or set of texts is followed by several questions. Select the best answer for each question and mark the letter (A), (B), (C), or (D) on your answer sheet.

Questions 147-148 refer to the following card.

Appointment Reminder

Department of Radiology

100 East Washington Street
Easton-Browning Hospital
Building J
Easton, MA 44590

Phone: 206-553-5500
Fax: 206-553-5501
E-mail: radiology@ebh.gov

**Browning
Medical
Clinic**

Just a friendly reminder about your upcoming appointment with

Dr. Seth Meyers

in our radiology clinic on <u>FEBRUARY 6</u> at 11:15 a.m.

Please give us a quick call at 206-553-5500 if you need to reschedule.

Note: Please refrain from eating three hours prior to your appointment.

---

147. For whom is the card intended?
(A) The Department of Radiology.
(B) Easton residents.
(C) Dr. Seth Meyers.
(D) A patient of Browning Medical Clinic.

148. What is the reader told NOT to do?
(A) Call the clinic to reschedule.
(B) Eat prior to the appointment.
(C) Arrive at 11:15 a.m.
(D) Park on Washington Street.

GO ON TO THE NEXT PAGE.

SEAFOOD KING

Weekly Specials

In **addition** to our regular menu, we serve the following daily specials

Monday	12.95
All you can eat deep-fried jumbo shrimp	
Tuesday	10.95
The King's special seafood gumbo	
Wednesday	13.95
Seafood sampler platter—a little of everything!	
Thursday Fish Fry	14.95
All you can eat golden fried perch	
Friday	17.95
Surf n' Turf—steak and lobster tail	

All specials served with soup, salad, and choice of 3 unlimited sides.

KING FOOD
GROUP, LLC

149. What can diners do if they don't want the daily special?
(A) Go somewhere else.
(B) Ask to speak with a manager.
(C) Create their own specials.
(D) Order from the regular menu.

150. What is NOT included with the daily specials?
(A) Soup.
(B) Salad.
(C) Side dishes.
(D) Beverages.

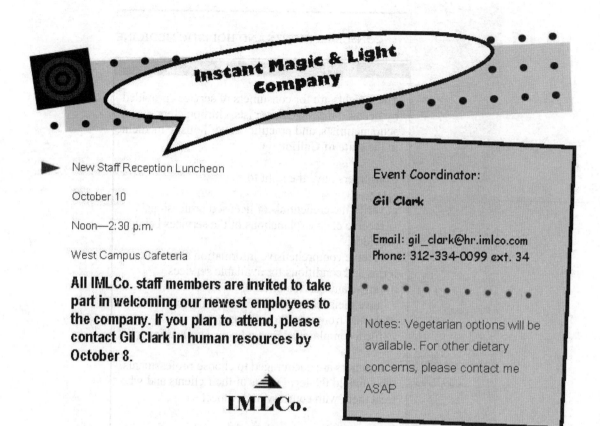

New Staff Reception Luncheon

October 10

Noon—2:30 p.m.

West Campus Cafeteria

All IMLCo. staff members are invited to take part in welcoming our newest employees to the company. If you plan to attend, please contact Gil Clark in human resources by October 8.

IMLCo.

Event Coordinator:

Gil Clark

Email: gil_clark@hr.imlco.com
Phone: 312-334-0099 ext. 34

Notes: Vegetarian options will be available. For other dietary concerns, please contact me ASAP

151. What is the purpose of the event?
- (A) To publicize new products.
- (B) To welcome new staff members.
- (C) To celebrate opening a new facility.
- (D) To recruit people for a job.

152. What should employees do if they want to attend the luncheon?
- (A) Apply for a position in the cafeteria.
- (B) Get in touch with Gil Clark.
- (C) Visit the West Campus Cafeteria on October 8.
- (D) Add their names to a waiting list.

GO ON TO THE NEXT PAGE.

CONSUMER RIGHTS AND HOLISTIC MEDICINE

These rights are for consumers of services provided by licensed massage therapists, chiropractors, acupuncturists, and practitioners of holistic medicine in the **state of California**.

Consumers have the right to:

- verify the credentials of licensed professionals.
- receive clear explanations of the services being provided.
- receive comprehensive information about rates, terms and conditions for available services.
- refuse any service offered.
- have their records and personal information protected from unauthorized use; and
- file a complaint against a licensed practitioner

Consumers are encouraged to choose professionals who uphold the legal rights of their clients and who treat them with courtesy and respect.

For more information about these rights or for a list of the services that licensed professionals may provide, please visit the Department of Economic Development, Consumer Advocacy Division, Room 33B, 1000 Throckmorton St., Sacramento, CA 92333, or call (208)392-1235 ext. 12.

Department of Economic
Development
Consumer Advocacy Division
Room 33B
1000 Throckmorton St.
Sacramento, CA 92333

Phone: (208) 392-1235
E-mail: advocate@ded.gov.ca

**The State of
California**

153. Why was the notice issued?
(A) To demonstrate effective ways to dispute a billing error.
(B) To announce a change in licensing regulations.
(C) To invite local professionals to a public hearing.
(D) To inform people of their legal rights.

154. What is implied about licensed service providers in the state of California?
(A) They must keep a file of complaints registered against them.
(B) They must show their certifications upon request.
(C) They are known for excellent consumer service.
(D) They reserve the right to refuse service to consumers.

Questions 155-157 refer to the following letter.

GLOBAL PASSPORT

Jethro Hastings
1202 Hal Greer Boulevard
Huntington, WV 25701

Re: Account # XXXX-XXXX-XXXX-7917
Amount $3,209.89

September 1

Dear Mr. Hastings,

Thank you for being a valued Global Passport customer. We apologize for an error concerning your Global Passport credit card account. On August 21, we issued a **temporary** credit to your account in the amount which you disputed on August 19. However, later, we accidentally issued another credit in the same amount to your account. To correct this error, we have withdrawn the surplus amount. The adjustment appears on the August statement, which was mailed today.

We **sincerely** regret any inconvenience this may have caused. If you have any questions or need further information, please visit us on the Web at www.gpcredit.com, or contact Customer Service at **1-888-903-2350** from 9:00 A.M. to 12 noon, Monday through Friday.

Regards,
Global Passport N.A.

Phone: 1-888-903-2350   Global Passport N.A.
1 Diamond Plaza
Newark, DE 23789   Orwell

---

155. What is the main purpose of this letter?
(A) To request additional documentation on a loan.
(B) To explain a policy on withdrawals.
(C) To inform someone of a correction to an account.
(D) To offer a special incentive program.

156. What happened on August 19?
(A) Mr. Hastings disputed a charge to his account.
(B) Mr. Hastings went over his credit limit.
(C) Global Passport issued a replacement card.
(D) Global Passport closed Mr. Hastings' account.

157. What is implied by the letter?
(A) An error was caught and corrected.
(B) The disputed charges may be considered valid.
(C) The account will be monitored for fraud.
(D) Mr. Hastings' can expect higher interest rates.

GO ON TO THE NEXT PAGE

From:	Yoon-see Kim <kim@gingersunlimited.com>
To:	Gordon Breesley <breesley@gingersunlimited.com>
Subject:	Safety Meeting
Date:	Tuesday, July 31, 4:01 P.M.

Gordon: If I'm not mistaken, we're scheduled to meet on Wednesday to discuss the company's recent safety performance, but I am afraid I have to reschedule. Tomorrow, Leslie Oberst from the Omaha office will be visiting us to talk about next year's advertising budget. Also, I'll be leaving for a trade show in Grand Rapids on Thursday, and then I'll be in Des Moines for a budget meeting on Friday. Can we reschedule for Monday? I will be back in Oklahoma City then. If this is not convenient for you, please let me know your availability for next week, and I'll try to work around your schedule. I'm very sorry for the last minute notice.

Yoon-see

158. What's the purpose of the e-mail?
(A) To inquire about an advertisement.
(B) To propose changes to a budget.
(C) To postpone a meeting.
(D) To make travel arrangements.

159. When will Yoon-see Kim meet with Leslie Oberst?
(A) On Monday.
(B) On Tuesday.
(C) On Wednesday.
(D) On Thursday.

160. Where does Gordon Breesley most likely work?
(A) In Omaha.
(B) In Grand Rapids.
(C) In Des Moines.
(D) In Oklahoma City.

Questions 161-164 refer to the following e-mail.

From:	Samuel Flynn <s_flynn@esusa_stl.com>
To:	Edge Scholastic St. Louis <allstaff@eestl.com>
Subject:	Prototype Testing
Date:	July 14, 11:22:01 CST

Dear Edge Scholastic Staff Members,

Our research and development team department has envi-
sioned a line of user-friendly school supplies for left-handed
students. As you know, most products on the market are designed for right-handers. We feel that there's a clear need for
a wider range of creative, high-quality left-centric products.

Currently we have three prototypes in the testing phase: scis-
sors, a notebook, and a computer mouse. Before these prototypes undergo formal product testing, we would like to conduct an internal survey here at the company. Therefore, we
would be very appreciative if employees volunteered to participate in a one-hour testing session during the week of July
21.

The testing session will take place in the R&D department on
the sixth floor of the Mooney Building. We need volunteers to
provide input on each prototype's comfort and ease of
use. Also, we are very interested in finding out whether these
prototypes are sufficiently different from other products already on the market. Needless to say, left-handed volunteers
are strongly urged to participate.

If you are interested in participating and are willing to volun-
teer your time during the week of July 21, please call Dina
Kashkari, Product Research Coordinator, at extension 45.

Thank you,
Samuel Flynn
Product Research Department

161. What is the main purpose of the e-mail?
(A) To solicit ideas for a new research project.
(B) To recruit employees to evaluate some prototypes.
(C) To share the results of a recent product testing.
(D) To survey employees about company policies.

162. According to the e-mail, what does the market need?
(A) Improved product testing procedures.
(B) An affordable line of durable office supplies.
(C) A greater variety of products for left-handed students.
(D) Creative product packaging.

163. What does Samuel Flynn wish to receive information about?
(A) Availability of product testing facility.
(B) Utility of some prototypes.
(C) Durability of some particular office supplies.
(D) The price of a newly marketed product.

164. What are interested people asked to do?
(A) Read some information.
(B) Make a call.
(C) Fill out a questionnaire.
(D) Send an e-mail.

GO ON TO THE NEXT PAGE

COLGATE PACKAGING INTERNATIONAL

ColPack Allied

Corporate HQ
489 West Arapahoe Rd.
Boulder, CO
80303

+1 303 382 1111
Fax: +1 303 382 1113
Web site: www.cpi.com

July 30
David Sweet
1716 N. Franklin Rd.
Broomfield, CO 80321

Dear Mr. Sweet,

I am pleased to offer you a position as senior account executive with CPI.

As we discussed during your interviews, you will be working at our new branch, in Broomfield, CO. You will report directly to Ms. Rooney, our regional manager.

You will receive a weekly salary of $2,500. Payroll is disbursed bi-weekly. Your compensation package also includes full medical and dental coverage, 10 days of medical and 20 days of personal leave. Contingent upon your completion of the first 90 days of employment, you will be eligible to enroll in our 401K program.

If this is acceptable to you, please sign and return the enclosed contract by Wednesday, August 5, either by fax or mail. Should you have any questions, feel free to contact me or Jill Ross, our director of human resources, at any time.

I am very confident that you will succeed in your role of managing our most valued and lucrative accounts.

Sincerely,

Orin Toth
Vice President of Operations

165. To whom will the new employee report?
(A) The supervisor of the travel department.
(B) The vice president of operations.
(C) The director of human resources.
(D) The regional manager.

166. What is Mr. Sweet asked to do?
(A) Travel to Idaho Falls.
(B) Sign and return a document.
(C) Contact the benefits department.
(D) Meet with Ms. Ross.

167. What is NOT mentioned as part of the compensation package?
(A) Personal time off.
(B) Medical and dental coverage.
(C) The 401K program.
(D) Housing stipend.

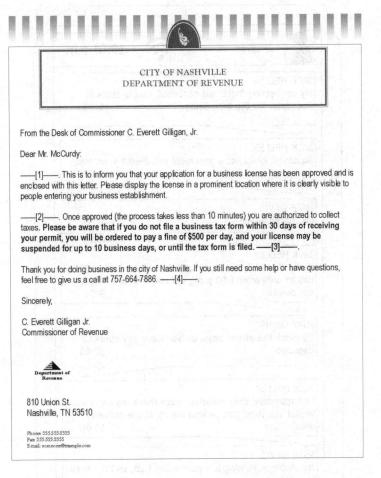

CITY OF NASHVILLE
DEPARTMENT OF REVENUE

From the Desk of Commissioner C. Everett Gilligan, Jr.

Dear Mr. McCurdy:

——[1]——. This is to inform you that your application for a business license has been approved and is enclosed with this letter. Please display the license in a prominent location where it is clearly visible to people entering your business establishment.

——[2]——. Once approved (the process takes less than 10 minutes) you are authorized to collect taxes. Please be aware that if you do not file a business tax form within 30 days of receiving your permit, you will be ordered to pay a fine of $500 per day, and your license may be suspended for up to 10 business days, or until the tax form is filed. ——[3]——.

Thank you for doing business in the city of Nashville. If you still need some help or have questions, feel free to give us a call at 757-664-7886. ——[4]——.

Sincerely,

C. Everett Gilligan Jr.
Commissioner of Revenue

Department of
Revenue

810 Union St.
Nashville, TN 53510

Phone: 555-555-5555
Fax: 555-555-5555
E-mail: someone@example.com

168. What information is announced in the letter?
(A) An office has been moved.
(B) A new tax law has been passed.
(C) A license has been issued.
(D) A previous letter was sent in error.

169. What does Mr. Gilligan ask Mr. McCurdy to do?
(A) Approve a request.
(B) Submit a form.
(C) Pay a late fee.
(D) Contact a local office.

170. The second paragraph, line 6, the word "suspended" is closest in meaning to?
(A) Interrupted.
(B) Organized.
(C) Purchased.
(D) Commanded.

171. In which of the positions marked [1], [2], [3] and [4] does the following sentence best belong?
"Now that you have received your business permit, please visit our Web site (http://www.Nashville.gov/index) to complete and submit the appropriate tax form electronically."
(A) [1]
(B) [2]
(C) [3]
(D) [4]

GO ON TO THE NEXT PAGE.

Questions 172-175 refer to the following message chain.

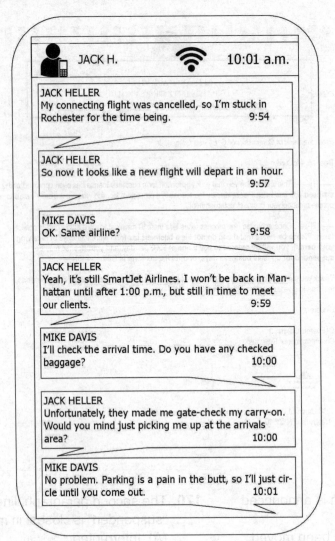

172. What is Jack Heller's problem?
(A) He missed his connecting flight.
(B) He forgot to book a hotel room.
(C) His flight was cancelled.
(D) The airline lost his luggage.

173. What is suggested about Jack Heller?
(A) He works for SmartJet Airlines.
(B) He is currently based in Rochester.
(C) He is on a business trip.
(D) He has been to Rochester more than once.

174. What does Jack Heller ask Mike Davis to do?
(A) Meet him at the office.
(B) Pick him up from the airport.
(C) Drop him off at the airport.
(D) Cancel the meeting.

175. At 10:01, what does Mike Davis mean when he says, "No problem"?
(A) He has confirmed the arrival time of the flight.
(B) He is certain he will be able to find a parking spot.
(C) He agrees to meet Mr. Heller at the arrivals area.
(D) He knows Jack Heller will be late.

Questions 176-180 refer to the following Web site and e-mail.

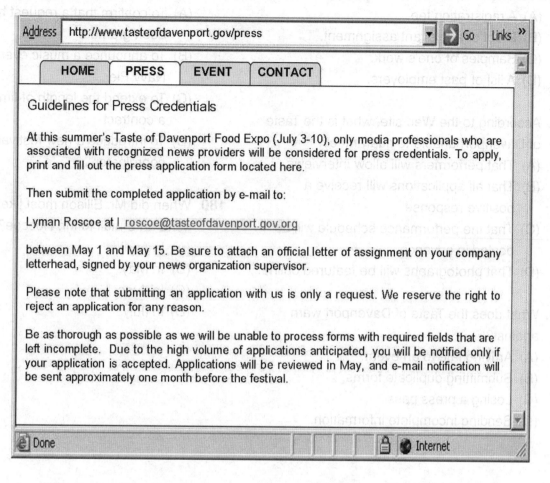

Address http://www.tasteofdavenport.gov/press ▼ 🔁 Go Links »

| HOME | PRESS | EVENT | CONTACT |

Guidelines for Press Credentials

At this summer's Taste of Davenport Food Expo (July 3-10), only media professionals who are associated with recognized news providers will be considered for press credentials. To apply, print and fill out the press application form located here.

Then submit the completed application by e-mail to:

Lyman Roscoe at l_roscoe@tasteofdavenport.gov.org

between May 1 and May 15. Be sure to attach an official letter of assignment on your company letterhead, signed by your news organization supervisor.

Please note that submitting an application with us is only a request. We reserve the right to reject an application for any reason.

Be as thorough as possible as we will be unable to process forms with required fields that are left incomplete. Due to the high volume of applications anticipated, you will be notified only if your application is accepted. Applications will be reviewed in May, and e-mail notification will be sent approximately one month before the festival.

🅴 Done 🔒 ● Internet

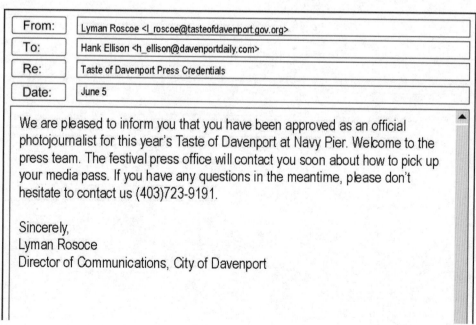

From:	Lyman Roscoe <l_roscoe@tasteofdavenport.gov.org>
To:	Hank Ellison <h_ellison@davenportdaily.com>
Re:	Taste of Davenport Press Credentials
Date:	June 5

We are pleased to inform you that you have been approved as an official photojournalist for this year's Taste of Davenport at Navy Pier. Welcome to the press team. The festival press office will contact you soon about how to pick up your media pass. If you have any questions in the meantime, please don't hesitate to contact us (403)723-9191.

Sincerely,
Lyman Rosoce
Director of Communications, City of Davenport

GO ON TO THE NEXT PAGE.

176. What must be included with the press form?
(A) A registration fee.
(B) Proof of a relevant assignment.
(C) Samples of one's work.
(D) A list of past employers.

177. According to the Web site, what is the Taste of Davenport unable to guarantee?
(A) That performers will allow interviews.
(B) That all applications will receive a positive response.
(C) That the performance schedule will be posted in advance.
(D) That photographs will be featured online.

178. What does the Taste of Davenport warn against?
(A) Arriving late to an event.
(B) Submitting duplicate forms.
(C) Losing a press pass.
(D) Sending incomplete information.

179. What is the purpose of the e-mail?
(A) To confirm that a request has been granted.
(B) To announce a music event at Navy Pier.
(C) To extend the length of time in a contract.
(D) To introduce a new festival coordinator.

180. When did Mr. Ellison most likely send an e-mail to Mr. Roscoe?
(A) In April.
(B) In May.
(C) In June.
(D) In July.

THE RECREATION CLUB

Relax!

Date: 08/22

Time: Noon—6:00 PM

Grand Opening in UPTOWN

Come visit our brand-new facility in Uptown!

As patrons of Recreation Clubs in Edgewater and Lakeview, you will soon have access to this amazing facility as part of your membership. This exclusive free preview event allows you to experience the club before everyone else.

Activities: Take a tour, taste samples of all cafe items, and meet our skilled instructors

Our grand opening for the general public will be held on Saturday, August 29. Come back for trial classes and more yummy treats. Some guests will receive complementary Recreation Club merchandise.

Highlights

- The Relax Cafe serves nutritious sanwiches, soda, and fruit drinks
- The indoor heated pool has separate areas for exercise and relaxation
- The Kid's Gym offers classes for children from 5 to 12 years old
- The Ultra Sport Room features bicycles with advanced digital monitors and controls — the first of their kind in the area

THE RECREATION CLUB

 Bradley Celdran: 212 237-0002

Recreation Clubs LLC

123 Hoover Boulevard
Cleveland, OH 56777

Phone: 212-237-0000
Fax: 212-237-0001
E-mail: info@therecclub.com

GO ON TO THE NEXT PAGE.

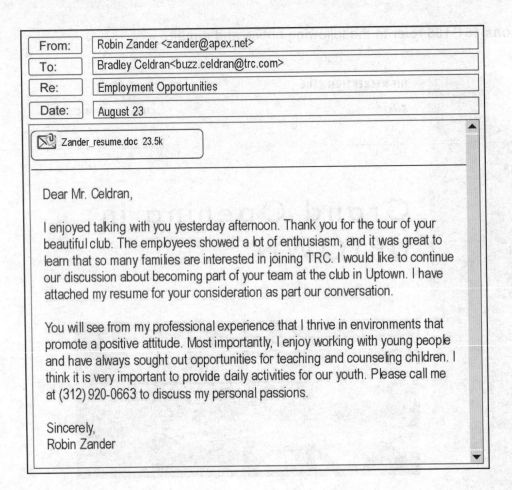

From:	Robin Zander <zander@apex.net>
To:	Bradley Celdran<buzz.celdran@trc.com>
Re:	Employment Opportunities
Date:	August 23

Zander_resume.doc 23.5k

Dear Mr. Celdran,

I enjoyed talking with you yesterday afternoon. Thank you for the tour of your beautiful club. The employees showed a lot of enthusiasm, and it was great to learn that so many families are interested in joining TRC. I would like to continue our discussion about becoming part of your team at the club in Uptown. I have attached my resume for your consideration as part our conversation.

You will see from my professional experience that I thrive in environments that promote a positive attitude. Most importantly, I enjoy working with young people and have always sought out opportunities for teaching and counseling children. I think it is very important to provide daily activities for our youth. Please call me at (312) 920-0663 to discuss my personal passions.

Sincerely,
Robin Zander

181. What will attendees do on August 22?
(A) Take a tour.
(B) Attend a seminar.
(C) Watch a video.
(D) Teach a class.

182. According to the notice, what is available only at the club in Uptown?
(A) Swimming lessons.
(B) Nutrition counseling.
(C) Discounted membership rates.
(D) Special exercise bicycles.

183. When did Ms. Zander most likely meet Mr. Celdran?
(A) During a scheduled job interview.
(B) During a hiring conference.
(C) During the club's preview event.
(D) During the club's grand opening.

184. To whom was the notice most likely sent?
(A) New residents of the Uptown area.
(B) People training to become exercise instructors.
(C) Current members of the Recreation Club.
(D) Commercial real estate investors.

185. Where in the club would Ms. Zander most likely wish to work?
(A) In the Relax Cafe.
(B) In the marketing department.
(C) In the Kid's Gym.
(D) In the Ultra Spin Room.

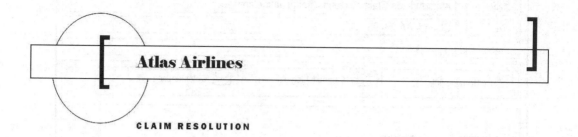

CLAIM RESOLUTION

Customer: COLEMAN, CANDY C.

33 Point Harbor Way

Orlando, FL 53333-9900

Ship To:

33 Point Harbor Way

Orlando, FL 53333-9900

Refund ID: #AA23499

Customer ID Code: colecan

Your Claim	Our Claim #	Approved	FOB	Ship Via	Terms	Tax ID
AA23499	JJ02389	Jeffcoat, K	AA9922	Standard	n/a	n/a

Atlas Airlines

Quant.	Claim Type	Item	Description	Standard Claim	Taxable	Unit Price	Total
1	Damaged	Bag	Standard Claim	135.00	n/a	n/a	135.00
1	Lost	Bag	Standard Claim	250.00	n/a	n/a	250.00
1	Issued	Voucher	Travel Voucher (6 Month)	100.00	n/a	n/a	100.00
						Subtotal	385.00
						Voucher	100.00

Atlas Airlines, Inc.
Central Baggage
4000 E Sky Harbor
Blvd.
Phoenix, AZ 85034
Fax 480-693-2305
Email: claims@aa.com

GO ON TO THE NEXT PAGE

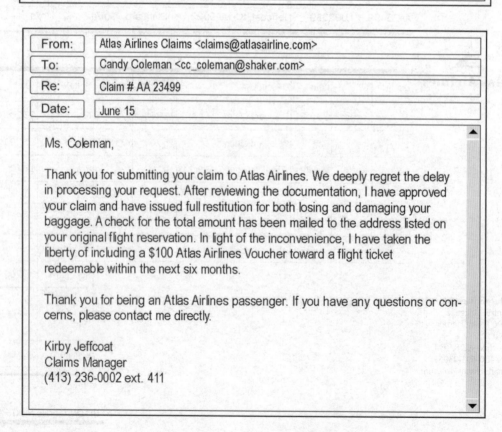

From:	Candy Coleman <cc_coleman@shaker.com>
To:	Atlas Airlines Claims <claims@atlasairline.com>
Re:	Claim # AA 23499
Date:	June 15

📩 Colecan.jpg 50k   📩 Coleman1.jpg 32k   📩 Coleman2.jpg 34k

To whom it may concern:

On May 19, I traveled from Newark, New Jersey, to Orlando, Florida, on Atlas Airlines Flight 810. My bag arrived on a different flight and was delivered to my home only a few hours ago. The contents were fine, but the exterior of the bag was badly damaged. The outside was dented. The suitcase is no longer usable as it cannot be closed properly. On May 21, I submitted claim form number AA 23499. I understood that it would take up to two weeks for the claim to be processed, but it is now June 15 and I have not had any response.

Please let me know how this problem will be resolved. As I did with the original claim, I am attaching a photo of the damaged property and photocopies of my boarding pass and baggage claim tickets.

Candy Coleman

From:	Atlas Airlines Claims <claims@atlasairline.com>
To:	Candy Coleman <cc_coleman@shaker.com>
Re:	Claim # AA 23499
Date:	June 15

Ms. Coleman,

Thank you for submitting your claim to Atlas Airlines. We deeply regret the delay in processing your request. After reviewing the documentation, I have approved your claim and have issued full restitution for both losing and damaging your baggage. A check for the total amount has been mailed to the address listed on your original flight reservation. In light of the inconvenience, I have taken the liberty of including a $100 Atlas Airlines Voucher toward a flight ticket redeemable within the next six months.

Thank you for being an Atlas Airlines passenger. If you have any questions or concerns, please contact me directly.

Kirby Jeffcoat
Claims Manager
(413) 236-0002 ext. 411

186. What does Ms. Coleman report about her bag?
- (A) It did not arrive with her flight.
- (B) It arrived at her home empty.
- (C) It was examined by airport personnel.
- (D) It was delivered to the wrong address.

187. When did Ms. Coleman most likely contact the claims department for the first time?
- (A) On May 19.
- (B) On May 21.
- (C) On June 15.
- (D) On June 25.

188. How much does Atlas Airlines typically pay for a lost bag?
- (A) $135.
- (B) $185.
- (C) $250.
- (D) $385.

189. Why did Kirby Jeffcoat reply to Ms. Coleman's email?
- (A) To inform her of a resolution to her claim.
- (B) To request more documentation to support her claim.
- (C) To confirm an address on her claim.
- (D) To follow up on a phone call related to her claim.

190. What did Atlas Airlines send to Ms. Coleman?
- (A) A check and a voucher.
- (B) A boarding pass.
- (C) A refund.
- (D) A claim ticket.

GO ON TO THE NEXT PAGE

Questions 191-195 refer to the following Web page, online form, and e-mail.

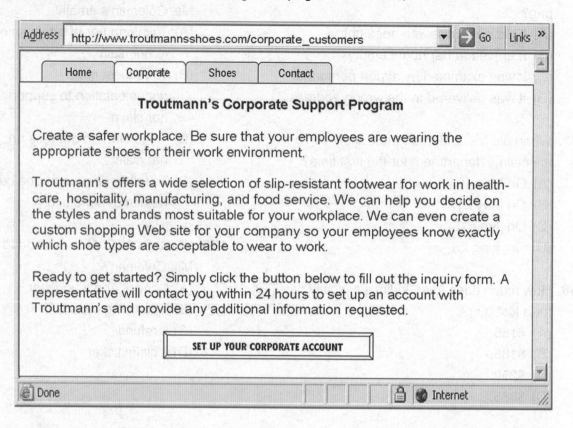

Address: http://www.troutmannsshoes.com/corporate_customers

| Home | Corporate | Shoes | Contact |

Troutmann's Corporate Support Program

Create a safer workplace. Be sure that your employees are wearing the appropriate shoes for their work environment.

Troutmann's offers a wide selection of slip-resistant footwear for work in health-care, hospitality, manufacturing, and food service. We can help you decide on the styles and brands most suitable for your workplace. We can even create a custom shopping Web site for your company so your employees know exactly which shoe types are acceptable to wear to work.

Ready to get started? Simply click the button below to fill out the inquiry form. A representative will contact you within 24 hours to set up an account with Troutmann's and provide any additional information requested.

SET UP YOUR CORPORATE ACCOUNT

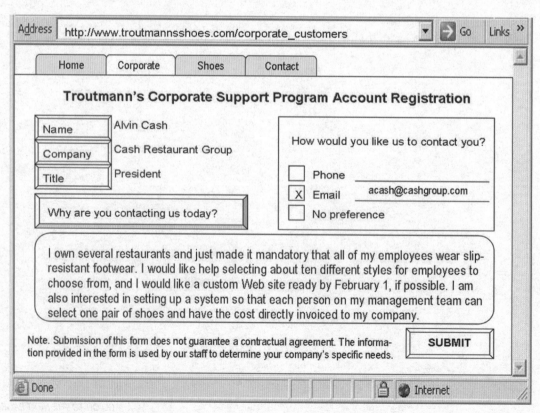

Address: http://www.troutmannsshoes.com/corporate_customers

| Home | Corporate | Shoes | Contact |

Troutmann's Corporate Support Program Account Registration

Name	Alvin Cash
Company	Cash Restaurant Group
Title	President

Why are you contacting us today?

How would you like us to contact you?

☐ Phone _____
☒ Email   acash@cashgroup.com
☐ No preference

I own several restaurants and just made it mandatory that all of my employees wear slip-resistant footwear. I would like help selecting about ten different styles for employees to choose from, and I would like a custom Web site ready by February 1, if possible. I am also interested in setting up a system so that each person on my management team can select one pair of shoes and have the cost directly invoiced to my company.

Note. Submission of this form does not guarantee a contractual agreement. The information provided in the form is used by our staff to determine your company's specific needs.

SUBMIT

From:	Dina Kowalski <corporate_accounts@troutmann.com>
To:	Alvin Cash <acash@cashgroup.com>
Re:	Your Account
Date:	January 26

Mr. Cash,

We appreciate your interest in Troutmann's Corporate Support Program. At this point, you are just a step away from setting up your account.

First of all, based on the information you submitted on our Web site, we are more than capable of accommodating your needs. Unfortunately, there may be a time-issue with your custom Web site. Our standard turnaround time for custom Web sites is generally 10 business days. However, if we act quickly, perhaps we can expedite the process to meet your requested deadline.

Please give me a call at your earliest convenience so we can discuss the terms and conditions of your account.

We look forward to working with you.

Dina Kowalski
Accounts Manager
(312)898-7733 ext. 11

191. To whom is the Web page directed?
(A) Accountants.
(B) Salespeople.
(C) Shoe designers.
(D) Business owners.

192. According to the form, what change recently occurred at Cash Restaurant Group?
(A) A new policy was implemented.
(B) A management team was hired.
(C) Several restaurants were sold.
(D) Employee uniforms were purchased.

193. What will Cash Restaurant Group employees probably be expected to do in February?
(A) Attend a safety workshop.
(B) Learn a new order-taking system.
(C) Make an online purchase.
(D) Work at a different location.

194. What service does Mr. Cash request that is NOT mentioned on the Web page?
(A) Recommending appropriate footwear.
(B) Setting up an account.
(C) Creating a custom Web site.
(D) Modifying a shoe design.

195. What problem does Ms. Kowalski mention in her e-mail?
(A) Mr. Cash has been banned from opening an account.
(B) She doesn't have ten different types of shoes.
(C) The company does not offer bulk discounts.
(D) The Web site may not be ready by February 1.

GO ON TO THE NEXT PAGE.

ROUSH POWER TOOLS

Milwaukee, Wisconsin

Phone: 800-211-0099
Fax: 888-919-2222
E-mail: contact@roush.com
http://www.roush.com

**Banks-Moore
Industries**

Roush XL-4 Cordless Power Drill

Roush XL-4 Cordless Drill has always had plenty of power. It now boasts new and improved features that make it the most versatile drill in its price range. With the updated design of the XL-4, you will feel confident tackling any home-improvement job from the heaviest task to the most delicate. Take a look at these exclusive features.

Balanced Handle - The XL-4's new ergonomic grip design features a non-slip surface and is shaped to fit your hand perfectly, minimizing fatigue.

Three-Speed Setting - In addition to the previous high and low setting. There is an extra-low speed setting for precision work. All three speeds work in forward and reverse, making it easy to match the best speed and direction for each drilling task.

Fan-Cooled Motor - Roush's patented fan-cooled system keeps the drill from overheating and decreases wear on the motor, greatly extending the drill's life.

Rechargeable battery - Our rapid-charge 18-volt battery now takes only two hours to fully charge. With the XL-4, you can return to your projects more quickly.

ROUSH POWER TOOLS

We build perfection.

ROUSH POWER TOOLS

Milwaukee, Wisconsin

Banks-Moore Industries

HOME | **PRODUCTS** | **SUPPORT** | **CONTACT**

Address: http://www.roush.com/products/reviews

User Reviews

Online User : Eduardo Garcia - San Dimas, CA
Customer Rating ★★★★☆ (four out of five stars)

My Roush XL-2 drill finally stopped functioning after years of use. When I learned about the updated product two weeks ago, I purchased it right away. The price was very reasonable, and I can honestly say that I have never used a better drill. While completing several different company projects, I was pleased to note that it works great for drilling into all kinds of wood. The handle on this new drill fits me much more comfortably, and it's remarkably light; my hand and wrist never get tired the way they did when I used the original model. I also like the slightly roomier storage case. If I have one complaint, it is that the redesigned motor with the fan is sometimes noisy and vibrates more than the motor in my previous drill. Overall though, the XL-4 is an improvement to what was already a good product.

XL-4 Cordless Power Drill

Modern Tool

Cordless Drill Comparison Chart

Modern Tool rounds up the newest models for a side-by-side comparison.

	Manufacturer/ Price	Model	Weight	Variable Speed	Battery	Max. Speed
	Roush $379	XL-4	3.8 lbs.	3-Speed	18.0v Slimpac Ion / 120 mins.	2000 rpm
	Clampett $279	CCD-330	4.2 lbs.	2-Speed	12.2v Nickel Ion / 60 mins.	1800 rpm
	Toledo $299	ODH-117	5.0 lbs.	2-Speed	15.5v Slimpac Ion / 90 mins.	1800 rpm

Compiled by Jack Tosh

Modern Tool

GO ON TO THE NEXT PAGE.

196. Where would the description be found?
- (A) In a directory of local companies.
- (B) In a training manual for a carpentry class.
- (C) On a Web site for home-improvement items.
- (D) In a brochure for a construction project.

197. What is suggested about the XL-4 drill?
- (A) It has a unique cooling system.
- (B) It is specially designed for professionals in the construction industry.
- (C) It features a traditional style handle.
- (D) Its price has never changed.

198. What is indicated about Mr. Garcia?
- (A) He used to be a Roush company associate.
- (B) He owned a Roush company product in the past.
- (C) He returned a product for a refund.
- (D) He recently built a house.

199. What new feature listed in the comparison chart does Mr. Garcia especially appreciate?
- (A) Nonslip grip.
- (B) Maximum speed.
- (C) Weight.
- (D) Price.

200. In the review, the word "model" in line 9, is closest in meaning to
- (A) pattern.
- (B) purpose.
- (C) example.
- (D) version.

Stop! This is the end of the test. If you finish before time is called, you may go back to Parts 5, 6, and 7 and check your work.

New TOEIC Listening Script

PART 1

1. (   ) (A) He is putting out a fire.
     (B) He is performing surgery.
     (C) He is giving a weather report.
     (D) He is sitting at a desk.

2. (   ) (A) The man is mopping the floor.
     (B) The man is painting the wall.
     (C) The man is washing the window.
     (D) The man is opening the door.

3. (   ) (A) Some people are shopping in a mall.
     (B) Some people are walking down a street.
     (C) Some people are swimming in a pool.
     (D) Some people are working in a factory.

4. (   ) (A) This is a bank.
     (B) This is a library.
     (C) This is a cafeteria.
     (D) This is an airport.

5. (   ) (A) The woman has just sold a car.
     (B) The woman has just sold a house.
     (C) The woman has just bought a dress.
     (D) The woman has just bought a desk.

6. (   ) (A) A house is being torn down.
     (B) A bridge is being built.
     (C) A boat is being towed.
     (D) A passenger is being rescued.

GO ON TO THE NEXT PAGE

PART 2

7. (   ) Where's the best place around here to grab a slice of pizza?

    (A) I think it could have been better.

    (B) Have you tried Sal's Pizzeria on Seventh Street?

    (C) A bag of potatoes.

8. (   ) Why are so many people coming in late today?

    (A) No, the deadline is next week.

    (B) I drive to work.

    (C) The transit workers went on strike.

9. (   ) Has your phone number changed in the past year?

    (A) No, there's no entry fee.

    (B) Yes, I switched carriers last month.

    (C) I left it at home.

10. (   ) Should I make a reservation at the Chinese restaurant or the Indian one?

    (A) Either one is fine with me.

    (B) Call the restaurant for directions.

    (C) I missed my flight.

11. (   ) When do we need to be at the airport?

    (A) In Singapore.

    (B) By seven-thirty.

    (C) Several times.

12. (   ) Did you happen to notice how many people signed up for the safety training session?

    (A) No, I didn't.

    (B) Mr. Fremont will.

    (C) The address is www.blacktie.com.

13. (   ) Would you like another piece of chocolate cake, Roger?

    (A) I think I have room for one more.

    (B) A table for three, please.

    (C) Yes, everything is quite expensive.

14. (   ) When is the music festival scheduled to begin?

    (A) Let's meet there.

    (B) It starts tomorrow.

    (C) No, I haven't.

15. (   ) Which platform does the Mountain Express depart from?
       (A) It was interesting.
       (B) It leaves from platform B.
       (C) There's one across the street.

16. (   ) Would you like to join us for coffee at the café in the lobby of our building?
       (A) That would be great.
       (B) Pasta, I think.
       (C) Yes, it's made of steel.

17. (   ) How long was Ms. Wagner on vacation?
       (A) It's too short.
       (B) At the doctor's office.
       (C) Only for a week.

18. (   ) Where do you want me to put all these progress reports?
       (A) Yes, take the elevator downstairs.
       (B) On my desk is fine.
       (C) The main office is being painted.

19. (   ) How long were the elevators out of commission?
       (A) At the airport.
       (B) About 500 dollars.
       (C) For six hours.

20. (   ) Have you ever been skydiving?
       (A) Yes, she's been there a long time.
       (B) No, I've never tried it.
       (C) It's closed for the season.

21. (   ) Who should we send the contract to?
       (A) All parties involved.
       (B) Print it on both sides.
       (C) By express mail.

22. (   ) What do you think of Mike and Steve co-managing the sales department?
       (A) Did she run there?
       (B) No, I'm off the rest of the week.
       (C) They make a good team.

GO ON TO THE NEXT PAGE.

23. (　　) If your computer seems to be running slow, close some of the programs you have open.
　　　(A) Thanks for the suggestion.
　　　(B) A short presentation.
　　　(C) It's today at two.

24. (　　) Can I help you find something in your size?
　　　(A) There's another seating at six.
　　　(B) I enjoyed it very much.
　　　(C) That would be great.

25. (　　) Wouldn't it be nice to visit Southern California this winter?
　　　(A) Yes, because it's a large facility.
　　　(B) It would. But we can't afford it.
　　　(C) Don't worry. Not until the last day of January.

26. (　　) Mr. Phelps said that the renovation project will only take a week.
　　　(A) I haven't decided yet.
　　　(B) We'll see about that.
　　　(C) We're moving next week.

27. (　　) Do you want to discuss the project now or after the meeting?
　　　(A) From the project manager.
　　　(B) Nothing for me, thanks.
　　　(C) Sorry, I'm busy right now.

28. (　　) What was the largest event your company has ever catered?
　　　(A) For the clearance sale at the Boston store.
　　　(B) We served twelve hundred people at a wedding.
　　　(C) It's a great food pairing, especially in the summer.

29. (　　) How many of these fliers do you think you're going to need?
　　　(A) Here, let me help you.
　　　(B) Sixty-five copies.
　　　(C) I don't know how to get there.

30. (　　) Why don't we stop by the pub later?
　　　(A) Sure, if you want to.
　　　(B) It stops at the corner.
　　　(C) Yes, half an hour.

46

31. (　　) Don't you have the same smart phone as Dave?

    (A) Yes, but mine is the latest model.

    (B) Sometimes I do.

    (C) I always call at that time.

PART 3

Questions 32 through 34 *refer to the following conversation between three speakers.*

Man A : Jenny and I are putting together the arrangements for the charity auction tomorrow, but we can't find any roses.

Man B : Our shipment never came from the greenhouse yesterday. We don't have any in stock.

W : Well , the client asked for pink and white roses, and we really need to start filling the vases today.

Man B : Relax, Jenny. I'll call our shop in Harrisburg and see if they can send us the flowers we need.

Man A : Worst comes to worst, I could run over to the supermarket and see what they have.

W : //Are you kidding? //We can't use supermarket flowers in our arrangements.

Man B: Actually, that's not a bad idea.

32. (　　) Where, most likely, do the speakers work?

    (A) At a post office.

    (B) At a catering business.

    (C) At a jewelry store.

    (D) At a flower shop.

33. (　　) What problem does the man mention?

    (A) A delivery did not arrive.

    (B) A customer made a complaint.

    (C) An employee was late.

    (D) A dinner was canceled.

34. (　　) What does the woman mean when she says, "Are you kidding?"?

    (A) She strongly disagrees.

    (B) She would like an explanation.

    (C) She feels disappointed.

    (D) She is pleasantly surprised.

GO ON TO THE NEXT PAGE.

M : So, Wendy, you've been here a few weeks now. How do you feel about the office atmosphere? Are you finding it productive?

W : Well, I'm used to working in an open office space, and I've never worked in a cubicle with high walls. So I feel isolated sometimes. Plus, the office is so quiet that it's almost distracting. Again, I'm used to having a lot of activity going on around me. I feed on that energy.

M : We used to have an open office floor plan, but now we collaborate and share ideas more easily over the inter-office network. Switching to a cubicle set-up took some time to get used to, but we've found it very beneficial in the long run.

W : I'm sure I'll adjust soon. And my supervisor told me it was OK to have a radio on as background noise. I think I'll try that next week.

35. (   ) What are the speakers mainly discussing?
    (A) A project proposal.
    (B) A work schedule.
    (C) A job opening.
    (D) An office layout.

36. (   ) What problem does the woman mention?
    (A) She has a long commute.
    (B) Renovations are very expensive.
    (C) She missed a deadline.
    (D) A work space is too quiet.

37. (   ) What will the woman probably do next week?
    (A) Transfer to another department.
    (B) Work longer hours.
    (C) Switch cubicles with another employee.
    (D) Listen to the radio while she works.

W : Hello, Mr. Morgan. I'm calling from Midnight Video. Our records show that you currently have a DVD overdue. The Adventures of Tom and Jerry should've been returned a week ago.

M : Yes, I know. I haven't finished watching it yet. Is it possible for me to get an extension on the rental?

W : I'm afraid not. There's a waiting list for that title, so it can't be renewed. There's also a fine of $5.00 per day the video I s overdue.

M : Ouch. Well, I guess I'll stop by this afternoon on my way to work to pay the fine and return the video.

38. (   ) Why is the woman calling?
    (A) A membership has expired.
    (B) A lost item was found.
    (C) An order has arrived.
    (D) A video is overdue.

39. (   ) What does the man ask about?
    (A) Applying for a job.
    (B) Renewing an item.
    (C) Taking a class.
    (D) Researching a topic.

40. (   ) What does the man plan to do this afternoon?
    (A) Give a presentation.
    (B) Pay the fine.
    (C) Take the day off.
    (D) Purchase a book.

Questions 41 through 43 *refer to the following conversation.*

M : Hi, Laurel. This is Damon Albarn calling from Saratoga Studios. I really want to thank you for coming to our offices yesterday, and leading the tutorial on the new CGI software.
W : It was my pleasure, Damon. The software's quite complicated but your employees have a very sharp learning curve.
M : I'm glad to hear that. And I've received nothing but positive feedback at my end. Unfortunately, some of our staff couldn't attend due to a scheduling conflict. I was hoping you could come back next week for a repeat performance?
W : Well, I'd be happy to come back, but I'll be at the consumer electronics show in Los Angeles all next week. Let's set something up for early next month.

41. (   ) What did woman do yesterday?
    (A) She updated a manual.
    (B) She inspected a facility.
    (C) She returned from a trip.
    (D) She taught a class.

GO ON TO THE NEXT PAGE.

42. (   ) What does the man ask the woman to do?
    (A) Repeat a tutorial.
    (B) Speak with her supervisor.
    (C) Send notes from a trade show.
    (D) Evaluate some software.

43. (   ) What problem does the woman mention?
    (A) She is missing a document.
    (B) She has not received a payment.
    (C) She is not available next week.
    (D) She does not know a password.

Questions 44 through 46 refer to the following conversation.

M : Hi, I saw your listing on Urban Habitat-dot-com for a two bedroom loft for rent on Mercer Street. I'm calling to find out when it's available.

W : We need a tenant who can move in on June first. It's a great living space. In fact, it's the only two-bedroom in the building that faces the river. The view is gorgeous. Would you like to schedule a time to see the place?

M : //For sure. //How about tomorrow in the early evening?

W : Why don't you come to the building tomorrow at 7:00 P.M.? I'll meet you by the front gate.

44. (   ) What does the man ask about the apartment?
    (A) How many rooms it has.
    (B) How much it costs.
    (C) When it is available.
    (D) Where it is.

45. (   ) What is unique about the apartment?
    (A) Its storage space.
    (B) Its architectural details.
    (C) Its scenic view.
    (D) Its upgraded appliances.

46. (   ) What does the man mean when he says, "For sure"?
    (A) He would like to see the apartment.
    (B) He would like to sign the contract.
    (C) He agrees to pay the deposit.
    (D) He knows where the apartment is located.

Woman A : I'm excited about Johnson's plan to bring in more customers. I previewed some of the advertisements for the upcoming campaign, and I think that will be really effective in attracting new business.

Woman B : Yes, I've seen them, too. You know, if we schedule to run print ads in June issues of selected magazines.

M : Right, and we launch the television ad campaign after that in July. But I hear there are still some discussions about whether to focus the television ads on Internet banking or home loans.

Woman A : There shouldn't even be a discussion. Our online banking system is the industry standard. I think that would appeal more to the type of customers we are looking for.

Woman B : And on television, they are really able to visualize all the features of the system.

47. (   ) What are the speakers mainly discussing?
    (A) The announcement of a new manager.
    (B) The introduction of a special service.
    (C) Plans for increasing business.
    (D) Procedures for a departmental process.

48. (   ) What will happen in July?
    (A) Television advertisements will be launched.
    (B) Client testimonials will be posted online.
    (C) A new Internet bank will be established.
    (D) An advertising agency will be hired.

49. (   ) What does Woman A say will appeal to customers?
    (A) Foreign currency exchange.
    (B) Extended business hours.
    (C) Home loans.
    (D) Online banking.

Questions 50 through 52 *refer to the following conversation and schedule.*

M : It's such a pleasure to finally meet you, Karen. As coordinator of this year's international trade conference, thank you for accepting our invitation to lead one of our sessions.

W : The pleasure is mine, Ralph. Our agency is always happy to have representatives participate in your conference.

GO ON TO THE NEXT PAGE.

M : As requested by your assistant, Cooper, your session has been scheduled for the afternoon of November 19. If you check the schedule, you will see the title of your presentation listed in the last time slot on that day.

W : Thank you very much, and I'll see you at the conference.

50. (　　) Who is the man?
    (A) An expert in international trade.
    (B) An event coordinator.
    (C) A trade representative.
    (D) An owner of an agency.

51. (　　) What has the woman agreed to do?
    (A) Lead a conference session.
    (B) Conduct an interview.
    (C) Schedule an appointment.
    (D) Accept a new position.

52. (　　) Look at the graphic. Who does the woman work for?
    (A) DuPree Logistics.
    (B) The Wilton Hotel.
    (C) Wolfgang Puck's Spoon.
    (D) Blackbox Associates.

International Trade Conference
Wilton Hotel, Baltimore, MD
Saturday, November 19

10:00 A.M. - 12:00 P.M.
"Transportation modes and how they can affect your supply chain"
Sponsored by DuPree Logistics – Drew Flint, Senior Partner
Meeting Room 101

12:00 Noon - 1:15 P.M.
Lunch
Wilton Hotel – Wolfgang Puck's Spoon

1:30 P.M. - 3:00 P.M.
"Asia: A strategic approach to your Asian marketing plan"
Sponsored by Blackbox Associates – Karen Hatrick, Chief Operating Officer
Meeting Room 102

3:15 P.M. - 4:00 P.M.
Closing Ceremony
Wilton Ballroom

M : Hey there, Lana. Didn't you recently start your own business designing Web sites for corporations? How is it going?

W : Well, it's been slow because at the beginning we were depending on referrals from friends and former co-workers. But last week we posted some advertising in a weekly trade journal, so I hope that'll bring us quite a bit more business.

M : Oh, that was a smart move. You know maybe I can help, too.

W : Really? How?

M : My department is interested in revamping our online shopping portal. I'd be happy to mention your company to my supervisor and suggest we hire you to design our new site.

W : That would be awesome!

53. (   ) What kind of business does the woman run?
      (A) A marketing firm.
      (B) A catering service.
      (C) An employment agency.
      (D) A web design company.

54. (   ) What does the man offer to do?
      (A) Help interview job candidates.
      (B) Review a budget.
      (C) Recommend the woman's business.
      (D) Write a resume.

55. (   ) Look at the graphic. How can potential customers receive a discount?
      (A) By mentioning the ad.
      (B) By presenting a coupon.
      (C) By signing up for a newsletter.
      (D) By placing an order before the end of the month.

PEERLESS WEB SERVICES
Custom Design and Support

Professional Web design services specializing in corporate and small business accounts

20% OFF

Visit our website to preview our work at **www.peerlessweb.com** *Mention this ad and receive 20% off your custom design package*

Tel: 712-333-0909
Ad Code: PWS-009

PWS

GO ON TO THE NEXT PAGE.

W : Hello, this is Rita Haywood. I dined at your restaurant last night, and I think I may have left my cellphone in the booth where we sat. Has it been located?

M : Yes, we found a cellphone, Ms. Heywood. It's locked in the manager's safe. He's not in his office yet but he'll certainly be here by noon today.

W : You guys are the best! Thank you. I'll drop by and pick it up this afternoon then.

M : No problem, but please remember to bring some kind of verification, like your cell phone bill. We'll have to see that before we can give you back the phone.

56. (   ) Why is the woman calling?
   (A) To ask about a missing item.
   (B) To discuss a seating arrangement.
   (C) To complain about a bill.
   (D) To cancel a reservation.

57. (   ) What does the man tell the woman to bring?
   (A) A bill.
   (B) A completed form.
   (C) A guest list.
   (D) A credit card.

58. (   ) Where will the woman most likely go this afternoon?
   (A) To a police station.
   (B) To a client's office.
   (C) To a restaurant.
   (D) To a bank.

Questions 59 through 61 *refer to the following conversation and list.*

W : Darryl, we have a new sales rep starting next month and we'll need to set her up with a PC and monitor. Can you place orders for those with our regular vendor?

M : Sure. You know CompCore has raised their prices, right?

W : No, I wasn't aware of that.

M : I just looked at the catalog a few minutes ago, and their current models are more expensive.

W : Right. Well, our budget per employee is $1,500 maximum. So let's order the system with the largest screen that falls within that price.

M : OK. I'll take a look at the prices again and place the order.

59. (   ) What does the woman ask the man to do?

    (A) Write a proposal.

    (B) Contact a job candidate.

    (C) Order some equipment.

    (D) Find a new vendor.

60. (   ) What problem does the man mention?

    (A) A computer model has been discontinued.

    (B) A departmental budget has been reduced.

    (C) A designer has left the company.

    (D) A supplier has increased its prices.

61. (   ) Look at the graphic. What size screen will the man order?

    (A) 15 inches.

    (B) 18 inches.

    (C) 21 inches.

    (D) 23 inches.

CompCore Product List
COMPUTER PACKAGES (INCLUDES MONITOR)

Screen Size	Price
SILVER Antel PC 866GHz processor 15" LCD monitor	$799
GOLD Antel PC 866GHZ processor 18" LCD monitor	$899
PLATINUM Antel PC 1.4GHz processor 18" LED monitor	$1099
PLATINUM PLUS Antel PC 1.4GHz processor 21" LCD monitor	$1199
DIAMOND Antel PC 2.2 GHZ processor 21" LED	$1299
DIAMOND PLUS Antel PC 2.2GHz processor 23" LCD	$1399

Questions 62 through 64 *refer to the following conversation and ad.*

M : Dr. Conroy, I have a question for you. I have an opening for a paid medical internship. And I know you just hired an intern last month. Where did you advertise the internship?

W : Well, I contacted Foster University School of Medicine and they recommended several students.

M : That's a good idea, except by now most of the students are on summer break. I really need the extra help as soon as possible.

W : Then maybe you should advertise the internship on MediLinks Web site. A lot of people use that website; doctors, nurses, and students. So you're sure to get a good number of applicants.

GO ON TO THE NEXT PAGE.

M : MediLinks, huh? Is it free to post an advertisement on the site?

W : No, you have to sign up for an account and there's a nominal fee, but it's well worth the investment.

62. (   ) What does the man want to do?
  (A) Hire an intern.
  (B) Write a paper.
  (C) Find a new job.
  (D) Conduct some research.

63. (   ) Why did the woman contact the university?
  (A) To sign up for a course.
  (B) To submit a research proposal.
  (C) To borrow the equipment.
  (D) To find qualified job applicants.

64. (   ) Look at the graphic. What is required for the internship?
  (A) A reliable vehicle.
  (B) A master's degree.
  (C) A grade point average of 3.0 or above.
  (D) A valid medical license.

If you are currently a medical student looking to make some extra money this summer, our leading medical research firm has openings for paid interns

Paid Medical Internship

Must have a GPA of 3.0 or higher and be currently enrolled in an accredited Pre-Med program

Facility is located in Foster City Transportation allowance provided for commuters

Tel: 413-356-7799

BioSearch Ltd.

Dr. Philip Baines

Questions 65 through 67 refer to the following conversation.

W : Greetings, I'm calling to ask about the aquarium's new summer hours. I heard that you'll be staying open late some evenings.

M : Yes, from May 31 until August 15 we will be open until 10:30 P.M. on Friday and Saturday nights. We are going to have special behind-the-scenes tours of the aquarium's facilities at that time.

W : That sounds neat! Is there an additional charge to join one of these tours?

M : No, the cost is included in the admission. However, we expect the aquarium will be quite crowded, so we suggest that you buy advance tickets on our Web site. That way you'll be able to avoid the lines.

65. (   ) Why is the woman calling?
    (A) To find out about a sale.
    (B) To sign up for membership.
    (C) To arrange a lecture.
    (D) To ask about a schedule.

66. (   ) What does the man recommend?
    (A) Checking an exhibit floor plan.
    (B) Arriving early to an event.
    (C) Signing up for a membership program.
    (D) Buying tickets online.

67. (   ) What is the aquarium going to offer during the summer?
    (A) Child care.
    (B) Interpretive dance lessons.
    (C) Free admission.
    (D) Special tours.

Questions 68 through 70 *refer to the following conversation and map.*

W : This is the faculty parking garage, right? Are you the guy who can issue a temporary parking permit?

M : I would be that guy, except we don't issue temporary permits for the faculty parking garage. However, I can issue a monthly parking permit for $75. I'll just need to see your university ID.

W : I'm a guest lecturer here. My name is Sondra McAllister. I'll be speaking at Woodside Hall.

M : You still need a permit to park here, Ms. McAlister.

W : But I'm only here for the week and wasn't issued a permit. Isn't there a parking policy in place to deal with visiting scholars?

M : Most use the public parking garage on University Avenue. There's a campus shuttle bus that will bring you back to Woodside Hall.

68. (   ) What does the woman request?
    (A) A different rental car.
    (B) A street map.
    (C) A bus schedule.
    (D) A temporary parking permit.

GO ON TO THE NEXT PAGE.

69. (   ) What does the man suggest?
    (A) Paying with a credit card.
    (B) Using an alternative parking area.
    (C) Selecting a smaller vehicle.
    (D) Rescheduling a lecture.

70. (   ) Look at the graphic. How far is Ms. McAllister from the Public Parking Garage right now?
    (A) One block.
    (B) Two blocks.
    (C) Three blocks.
    (D) Four blocks.

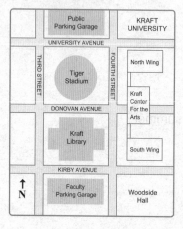

PART 4

Questions 71 through 73 refer to the following excerpt from a meeting.

Thanks for inviting me here today. Your firm already uses solar panels for alternative energy on new architectural projects. So I think you'll be very interested in our company's latest product—the TED Real-Time Energy Monitor. This device measures the electrical output of solar panels and converts usage to dollar amounts, so it gives users a clear idea of how much money they'll save on energy costs each day. Since you've been hired to design the new Robinson Center for the Arts next year, this monitoring system will be an attractive feature to your clients. Now let me pass around some information about the technical specifications of this product.

71. (   ) What is the purpose of the speaker's visit?
    (A) To present research findings.
    (B) To promote a new product.
    (C) To improve worker efficiency.
    (D) To explain a corporate procedure.

72. (   ) According to the speaker, what are the listeners planning to do next year?
   (A) Open an overseas office.
   (B) Design a building.
   (C) Restructure a department.
   (D) Host a trade show.

73. (   ) What will the speaker most likely do next?
   (A) Answer some questions.
   (B) Distribute some documents.
   (C) Introduce a guest.
   (D) Complete an installation.

Questions 74 through 76 *refer to the following telephone message.*

Hello, Mr. Yearling? This is Janet Loeb from Sonic Boom Beverages. The marketing team listened to the jingle you wrote for our radio advertisement for our new all-natural energy drinks. We really like the song and think that it will appeal to our target audience. Our only concern is that our product name is not repeated at the end of the song. Can you please record a new version? Once you've done that, we should be able to use it in our advertisement.

74. (   ) What product is being discussed?
   (A) An energy drink.
   (B) A vitamin supplement.
   (C) A breakfast cereal.
   (D) A nutrition bar.

75. (   ) What concern does the caller mention?
   (A) A product name is not repeated.
   (B) A focus group did not like a flavor.
   (C) A song is too long.
   (D) A package is difficult to open.

76. (   ) What does the speaker request that the listener do?
   (A) Send additional samples.
   (B) Come to the company headquarters.
   (C) Suggest another name.
   (D) Record a song again.

GO ON TO THE NEXT PAGE.

Questions 77 through 80 *refer to the following broadcast.*

Good evening. First up on Space Tonight, we have news of an exciting discovery made near the edge of the Milky Way. A team of astronomers have found a black star that's never been observed by experts before. They're trying to find a name for the star and they're asking the public to submit ideas. Later on the program, we'll tell you how to enter the contest on our website and have a chance to win a trip to the Aldren Space Center in Cocoa Beach. But first, we'll hear from Dr. Gabriel Dyson, the lead astronomer on the team. He's here in the studio with us to talk to us about this truly fascinating discovery.

77. (   ) What is the broadcast mainly about?
  (A) An international award.
  (B) A scientific discovery.
  (C) A sports competition.
  (D) An upcoming conference.

78. (   ) According to the speaker, what can listeners do on a Web site?
  (A) Read an article.
  (B) Enter a contest.
  (C) Check program listings.
  (D) View photographs.

79. (   ) Who is Dr. Gabriel Dyson?
  (A) A tour guide.
  (B) An astronomer.
  (C) A journalist.
  (D) A nutritionist.

Questions 80 through 82 *refer to the following talk.*

On behalf of the legal team here at Rice Faber, I'd like to welcome you to the firm. Now I know you're all certified legal assistants, but we want to make sure you feel comfortable with your assignments. So for your first week, you'll be assigned a mentor. These experienced staff members will explain our procedures and answer questions you have about the firm. At the end of the week, your mentor will evaluate your work and let us know if you're ready to handle assignments independently. We're very happy you're here and we hope you enjoy the work.

80. (　　) Who is the intended audience of the talk?
　　　　(A) Computer repair technicians.
　　　　(B) Customer service representatives.
　　　　(C) Financial advisers.
　　　　(D) Legal assistants.

81. (　　) How will listeners be trained?
　　　　(A) By watching online videos.
　　　　(B) By attending a series of workshops.
　　　　(C) By reading an employee handbook.
　　　　(D) By working with experienced employees.

82. (　　) What does the speaker say will happen at the end of the week?
　　　　(A) New employees will be evaluated.
　　　　(B) Participants will attend a banquet.
　　　　(C) Policies will be updated.
　　　　(D) Schedules will be posted.

Questions 83 through 85 refer to the following announcement and graphic.

Hi, everyone. I hope you're enjoying the conference. Um, before we get started with the next presentation, I have a quick announcement. You should have received the prepaid vouchers for the welcome dinner tonight in your registration packet. But it looks like some of the packets were missing them. So if you didn't get one, I'll be in the lobby distributing vouchers during the break at 3 o'clock. You just need to present your conference badge in order to receive your voucher. So don't forget it. Okay?

83. (　　) Who most likely are the listeners?
　　　　(A) Concert performers.
　　　　(B) Technical support staff.
　　　　(C) Conference attendees.
　　　　(D) Restaurant servers.

84. (　　) What problem does the speaker mention?
　　　　(A) A room has not been reserved.
　　　　(B) Some tickets were not distributed.
　　　　(C) A speaker is unavailable.
　　　　(D) A microphone is not working.

GO ON TO THE NEXT PAGE

85. (　　) Look at the graphic. Where will the dinner be held?
    (A) In a cafeteria.
    (B) In a conference room.
    (C) In a hotel ballroom.
    (D) In a casual restaurant.

AVIDENT BUSINESS CONFERENCE

WELCOME DINNER

VOUCHER

Good for one (1) registered attendee

Date: Tuesday, January 15
Time: 6:30 p.m.
Location: Regent Hotel, Silverbox Ballroom
Please present this voucher upon arrival

Questions 86 through 88 refer to the following telephone message.

Hey, there, Michelle. This is George calling from Phoenix. Competition just wrapped up at the karate tournament here. Unfortunately, our flight home has been delayed. I'm really sorry, but this means I won't be able to make it to the regional athletic association meeting tomorrow. I know you were counting on me to represent our school at the meeting, and to vote for a new association chairperson. Do you think you could go in my place instead? Anyway, I'm very pleased with how well our team did at the tournament. We had six kids finish in the top three of their weight class. But I'll tell you all about it when I get back.

86. (　　) Where does the speaker most likely work?
    (A) At a local airport.
    (B) At a fitness magazine.
    (C) At a martial arts school.
    (D) At a travel agency.

87. (   ) Why does the speaker apologize?
    (A) He has missed a publication deadline.
    (B) He has misplaced a set of keys.
    (C) He is unable to attend a meeting.
    (D) He cannot access a computer network.

88. (   ) What is the speaker pleased about?
    (A) The features of a new software system.
    (B) The changes to an advertising budget.
    (C) The number of people at an event.
    (D) The performance of some team members.

Questions 89 through 91 _refer to an excerpt from a meeting and survey results._

The next thing I'd like to discuss during our meeting today is the result of the survey that library patrons filled out in the past month. One thing we were surprised by was the comments and feedback about the wait time at the information desk. A number of people reported being frustrated because there isn't enough staff. So we'll definitely need to hire more staff. //On a positive note, //I'm happy to say that our idea for possibly hosting a weekly movie night seemed to appeal to our patrons. If we do go ahead with this idea, they'd like to see a variety of genres including documentaries and international films.

89. (   ) Look at the graphic. What are library patrons most pleased with?
    (A) Renewal policies.
    (B) Overall selection.
    (C) Ease of access to materials.
    (D) Wait times at the information desk.

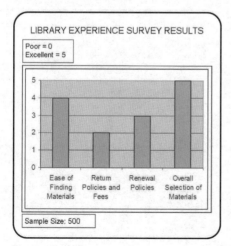

90. (   ) What does the woman mean when she says, "On a positive note"?
     (A) She will answer some questions.
     (B) She wants the listeners to take notes.
     (C) She will introduce a different subject.
     (D) She has more bad news for the listeners.

91. (   ) What does the speaker say about the library's information desk?
     (A) It is understaffed.
     (B) It is being repaired.
     (C) It has recently been relocated.
     (D) It will get a faster Internet connection.

Questions 92 through 94 *refer to the following broadcast.*

It wouldn't be Declaration Day in Point Howard without the annual firework show, which made its debut in 1901 to commemorate the city's founding. The all-day event takes place this Sunday on the Boardwalk at Point Howard and includes carnival rides, games, food and a free concert. The fireworks display will be set off from barges in the harbor. Usually, the best views are from the north side of the point; however, Seventh Street Trail is closed for on-going maintenance. So the best viewing spot will be from the beach. If you plan on heading to where the action is, arrive early to grab a good spot. A large crowd is expected, so pack blankets or chairs and enjoy the party. You can check our website for a map of more favorite spots to watch the fireworks.

92. (   ) Look at the graphic. Where will the listeners be unable to go on Sunday?
     (A) The Boardwalk.
     (B) The Picnic Area.
     (C) Harbor Point Road.
     (D) Sunset Beach.

93. (   ) What is said about the beach?
    (A) It will be under construction.
    (B) It will cost money to cross.
    (C) It will be closed to traffic.
    (D) It will provide a good view.

94. (   ) What is scheduled for Sunday?
    (A) A sporting event.
    (B) A city celebration.
    (C) A local election.
    (D) A walking tour.

Questions 95 through 97 refer to the following announcement.

Attention, passengers of Concordia Airlines flight 2424 with service to Burbank. We apologize for the delay while the aircraft is being refueled. But we are now ready to begin boarding. It's going to be a full flight. So I need to remind everyone about our baggage regulations. Each passenger is allowed only one carry-on item of no more than 15 pounds. Any items weighing more than that or additional luggage will have to be checked here at the desk. At this point, we are only boarding those passengers with small children and those who need assistance. In a few minutes, we'll begin boarding rows 40 through 55. Please take out your boarding passes for inspection to speed up the process.

95. (   ) What does the speaker remind listeners of?
    (A) A transfer procedure.
    (B) Luggage restrictions.
    (C) A frequent-flier program.
    (D) In-flight meal options.

96. (   ) What was the cause of the delay?
    (A) An airplane was undergoing a routine check.
    (B) There was heavier air traffic than expected.
    (C) An airplane needed more fuel.
    (D) There was bad weather in the area.

GO ON TO THE NEXT PAGE

97. (   )   What does the speaker request that listeners do?
          (A) Move to a different waiting area.
          (B) Accept new seat assignments.
          (C) Claim their belongings.
          (D) Have their boarding passes ready.

Questions 98 through 100 refer to the following advertisement.

The Work Bench offers the highest quality brands for your home improvement needs, so don't miss out on our blowout discount event. If you think our products are too expensive for you, think again. This Monday only, mention this ad, and when you buy one Solarais® Portable Chain Saw at $299.99, and get the second at 50 percent off the retail price. If transportation of larger boxes is an issue, don't worry. We can ship your purchase directly to your home at no additional cost. See you at the Work Bench this Monday.

98. (   )   What type of merchandise is being advertised?
          (A) Hardware.
          (B) Small electronics.
          (C) Packing materials.
          (D) Clothing.

99. (   )   How can customers receive a discount on Monday?
          (A) By purchasing larger boxes.
          (B) By referring to an advertisement.
          (C) By presenting a coupon.
          (D) By opening a line of credit.

100. (   )   According to the speaker, what additional service does the store provide?
          (A) Orders are shipped free of charge.
          (B) Representatives are available 24 hours a day.
          (C) Customers can preorder merchandise.
          (D) Gift wrapping is complimentary with every purchase.

NO TEST MATERIAL ON THIS PAGE

GO ON TO THE NEXT PAGE.

New TOEIC Speaking Test

Question 1: Read a Text Aloud

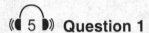 **Question 1**

Directions: In this part of the test, you will read aloud the text on the screen. You will have 45 seconds to prepare. Then you will have 45 seconds to read the text aloud.

You don't need to spend all of your hard earned money on coffee. Making your own cappuccino at home is easy with the new Cappuccino Wizard by Rossi. Unlike other espresso machines that can be difficult to clean and maintain, the Cappuccino Wizard breaks down into five parts that can go directly into your dishwasher. This stainless steel appliance will brew a cup of coffee for you in a fraction of the time it takes to travel to the nearest café.

PREPARATION TIME
00 : 00 : 45

RESPONSE TIME
00 : 00 : 45

Question 2: Read a Text Aloud

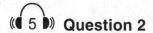 **Question 2**

Directions: In this part of the test, you will read aloud the text on the screen. You will have 45 seconds to prepare. Then you will have 45 seconds to read the text aloud.

There is a belief among packaging experts that shoppers can be convinced to buy a product if the package that contains the product appeals to the senses. Designers have spent years testing packages, doing market research studies, and logging the reactions of various target groups, just to come up with the perfect product package. Color plays a very important role in determining the best direction to go with packaging.

PREPARATION TIME
00 : 00 : 45

RESPONSE TIME
00 : 00 : 45

GO ON TO THE NEXT PAGE.

Question 3: Describe a Picture

Directions: In this part of the test, you will describe the picture on your screen in as much detail as you can. You will have 30 seconds to prepare your response. Then you will have 45 seconds to speak about the picture.

PREPARATION TIME
00 : 00 : 30

RESPONSE TIME
00 : 00 : 45

Question 3: Describe a Picture

答題範例

 **Question 3**

Three people are in the water with three dolphins.

There are two women and one man.

They appear to be wearing wetsuits.

The gender of the dolphins cannot be determined.

The people and the dolphins have formed a circle.

The people are holding the dolphins by their fins, as
   if they were holding hands.

The dolphins also appear to be poised on their tails,
with their snouts pointed toward the sky.

This is apparently some kind of learned trick or
   performance.

The people are smiling but it is impossible to say
   what the dolphins are feeling at this point.

I suspect this may be part of some kind of water show.

They have trained the dolphins to perform with the
   humans.

GO ON TO THE NEXT PAGE

Questions 4-6: Respond to Questions

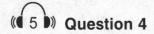 **Question 4**

Directions: In this part of the test, you will answer three questions. For each question, begin responding immediately after you hear a beep. No preparation time is provided. You will have 15 seconds to respond to Questions 4 and 5 and 30 seconds to respond to Question 6.

A nutritionist is doing research in your area. You have agreed to participate in an interview about food. Do you cook at home or take most of your meals outside?

Question 4
Why do you cook at home?

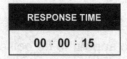

Question 5
Where do you do most of your shopping?

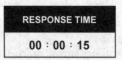

Question 6
Describe your favorite dish to prepare.

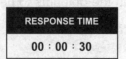

Questions 4-6: Respond to Questions

答題範例

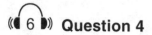 **Question 4**

Why do you cook at home?

Answer

> I prefer to cook at home for several reasons.
>
> First of all, it's cheaper than eating out.
>
> Second, it's generally more nutritious.

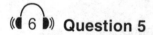 **Question 5**

Where do you do most of your shopping?

Answer

> There isn't one particular place.
>
> I shop at both supermarkets and local markets.
>
> I go wherever there is a sale.

GO ON TO THE NEXT PAGE.

Questions 4-6: Respond to Questions

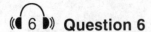 **Question 6**

Describe your favorite dish to prepare.

Answer

My favorite dish to prepare is an Italian dish called

fettuccini alfredo.

It's pasta in a white cream sauce.

It's very rich and flavorful.

First, you make the sauce with butter and cream.

Then you boil the pasta.

When it's ready, you combine the pasta and sauce.

Questions 7-9: Respond to Questions Using Information Provided

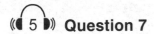 **Question 7**

Directions: In this part of the test, you will answer three questions based on the information provided. You will have 30 seconds to read the information before the questions begin. For each question, begin responding immediately after you hear a beep. No additional preparation time is provided. You will have 15 seconds to respond to Questions 7 and 8 and 30 seconds to respond to Question 9.

Hi, this is Emily Foster. I'm calling about a flyer I saw posted at the supermarket. I was wondering if you could answer a few questions for me?

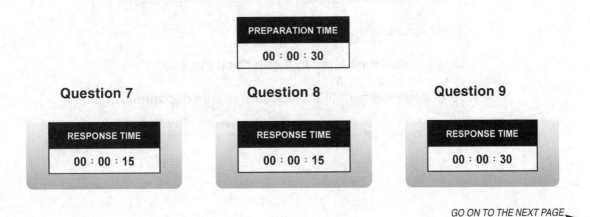

GO ON TO THE NEXT PAGE

Questions 7-9: Respond to Questions Using Information Provided

答題範例

 Question 7

When and where is the car wash being held?

Answer

> The car wash is this Saturday, July 10.
>
> It lasts from 8:00 a.m. to 5:00 p.m.
>
> It is being held in Parking Lot B at Jenner High School.

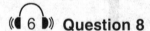 Question 8

Who is hosting the car wash?

Answer

> The car wash will be hosted by the Jenner High School
>
>   Thespian Society.
>
> These are kids interested in theater and the arts.
>
> All proceeds will benefit the school's drama department.

Questions 7-9: Respond to Questions Using Information Provided

 **Question 9**

How much would it cost to have my SUV washed?

Answer

> There is no fixed price for a car wash.
>
> However, there is a recommended donation of 10
>
> dollars.
>
> You could always pay more if you want.
>
>
> Most people give the recommended donation.
>
> Meanwhile, there will be free snacks and drinks.
>
> Hope to see you there!

GO ON TO THE NEXT PAGE.

Question 10: Propose a Solution

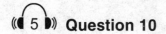 **Question 10**

Directions: In this part of the test, you will be presented with a problem and asked to propose a solution. You will have 30 seconds to prepare. Then you will have 60 seconds to speak. In your response, be sure to show that you recognize the problem, and propose a way of dealing with the problem.

In your response, be sure to

- show that you recognize the caller's problem, and
- propose a way of dealing with the problem.

PREPARATION TIME
00 : 00 : 30

RESPONSE TIME
00 : 01 : 00

Question 10: Propose a Solution

答題範例

 **Question 10**

Voice Message

> Hi, this is Dr. Leonard Tobin. I made dinner reservations for three people at 7:45 p.m. this evening, and I'd like to change that number to five. Because it's a Friday night, I was told by the hostess that someone from the restaurant would call and confirm this reservation, but I never heard back from you. At the same time, I asked specifically to be seated at table 10 in the main dining room; however, I'm aware that it only seats four. If it isn't possible to squeeze in a fifth person, I'd like to waive that request and note that any table in the main dining room would be suitable. I'd appreciate it if you could please call me back and confirm the new reservation as soon as possible. I can be reached at 444-2323. Thank you and have a nice day.

GO ON TO THE NEXT PAGE.

Question 10: Propose a Solution

答題範例

Hello, Dr. Tobin.

This is Mary from Indian Palace Restaurant.

I have received your message.

First, please accept my apologies for not getting back to you in a
   timely manner.

We have been experiencing a very high volume of phone calls today.

Anyway, it was I who took your original reservation.

I have you in the books for three people at 7:45.

Also noted is your request for table 10 in the main dining room.

I understand that you wish to change this reservation.

I will most likely be able to accommodate your request to increase
   your party from three to five.

However, it's not likely that I can seat you in the main dining room.

Actually, the second seating in main dining room is completely
   overbooked tonight.

On the other hand, I do have tables available on the patio.

There are a few tables available in the lounge area as well.

Also, if you would be willing to change your reservation to 9:15,
   I could put you in the main dining room.

Please give me a call at your earliest convenience.

Hopefully, we can come to a mutually beneficial compromise.

I can be reached here at 927-0033.

Question 11: Express an Opinion

 **Question 11**

Directions: In this part of the test, you will give your opinion about a specific
topic. Be sure to say as much as you can in the time allowed.
You will have 15 seconds to prepare. Then you will have 60
seconds to speak.

Some companies make donations to local charities and community
groups. Other companies do not and leave it up to their staff to decide
whether to make personal donations. Should companies donate part of their
profits to charities? State your opinion and provide reasons for your view.

PREPARATION TIME
00 : 00 : 15

RESPONSE TIME
00 : 01 : 00

GO ON TO THE NEXT PAGE

Question 11: Express an Opinion

答題範例

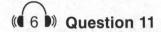 **Question 11**

Generally speaking, I think it's up to the company.

I don't believe any organization should be forced or compelled to be charitable.

That goes for employees as well.

On the other hand, a company may choose to create some kind of charitable foundation that is not strictly profit-based.

In fact, some companies have charity tied in to their general fiscal plan.

Microsoft, for example, has several charitable programs that are not related to their profit margin.

That may be because charitable donations are tax-deductible.

Many companies are eager to donate money to ease their tax burden.

That type of accounting isn't exactly "charitable" but it probably does some good in the world.

However, if I were working for a company that decided to give millions of dollars to a non-profit organization that fights to eradicate malaria in the Congo instead of giving its employees a five percent raise, I wouldn't stay at that company for very much longer.

It's not that I'm pro-malaria in the Congo; it's that I don't appreciate having my personal finances dictated by any type of authority.

It's akin to theft.

If the company had instead come to us (the staff) and said, "Hey, what do you think about this idea?" then perhaps I might be willing to compromise.

For instance, give us a three percent raise and give the balance to charity.

That's a bit more reasonable.

Meanwhile, not everybody can agree on a worthwhile cause, and that's terrible from a business perspective.

You want everybody on the same page.

By choosing one particular charity, you run the risk of alienating people with other causes closer to their hearts.

That can cause division and upset company morale.

That leads to other problems like low performance and high employee turnover.

No, I think it's best if a company doesn't involve its employees in corporate charity.

GO ON TO THE NEXT PAGE.

NO TEST MATERIAL ON THIS PAGE

New TOEIC Writing Test

Questions 1-5: Write a Sentence Based on a Picture

Question 1

Directions: Write ONE sentence based on the picture using the TWO words or phrases under it. You may change the forms of the words and you may use them in any order.

pool / laps

GO ON TO THE NEXT PAGE.

Questions 1-5: Write a Sentence Based on a Picture

Question 2

Directions: Write ONE sentence based on the picture using the TWO words or phrases under it. You may change the forms of the words and you may use them in any order.

woman / couch

Questions 1-5: Write a Sentence Based on a Picture

Question 3

Directions: Write ONE sentence based on the picture using the TWO words or phrases under it. You may change the forms of the words and you may use them in any order.

bus / open

Questions 1-5: Write a Sentence Based on a Picture

Question 4

Directions: Write ONE sentence based on the picture using the TWO words or phrases under it. You may change the forms of the words and you may use them in any order.

dishes / kitchen

Questions 1-5: Write a Sentence Based on a Picture

Question 5

Directions: Write ONE sentence based on the picture using the TWO words or phrases under it. You may change the forms of the words and you may use them in any order.

ferry / waiting

GO ON TO THE NEXT PAGE

Questions 6-7: Respond to a written request

Question 6

Directions: Read the e-mail below.

From:	Joe Prietoriou <jprietoriou@opportunity.com
To:	Chris Thomas <chris.thomas.jr@opportunity.com
Re:	Employers Are Looking For YOU!
Date:	October 30 11:11:34 EST

Hi, Chris. I did not intentionally ignore your last message. I haven't been using this Web site for recruiting purposes as of late. Please feel free to contact me if you are interested in discussing employment opportunities further.

Regards,
Joe Pretoriou
JP Recruiting Associates

Directions: Write to Joe as Chris and first, thank him for responding to you. Then tell him how you feel about discussing his employment opportunities. Provide at least one detail to support your response.

Questions 6-7: Respond to a written request

答題範例

Question 6

From:	Chris Thomas <chris.thomas.jr@opportunity.com
To:	Joe Prietoriou <jprietoriou@opportunity.com
Re:	Employers Are Looking For YOU!
Date:	November 1 20:02:51 EST

Hi, Joe. Thanks for getting back to me. I understand how these things go. Anyway, I'd certainly be interested in discussing potential employment opportunities; however, in the time that has lapsed since I first contacted you, I have found a position with Johnson Industries. I'm happy here and have no plans to leave, but it's always good to keep one's options open. If there is an opening for which you think I would be particularly suited, by all means, please let me know.

Best,
Chris Thomas

GO ON TO THE NEXT PAGE.

Questions 6-7: Respond to a written request

Question 7

Directions: Read the e-mail below.

From:	Hilda Burkhart <hilda@burkhartrentals.com
To:	Ron Swanson <r_swanson@latimes.com
Re:	Unpaid Rentals for Unit 7-B Mandarin Gardens
Date:	February 12

Dear Mr. Swanson:

I wish to inform you (as a co-signor of the lease contract (for Unit 7-B, Mandarin Garden Homes), that you and your wife Ms. Carol Swanson have not paid the rent since January 10, or equivalent to two months unpaid now. She said she would pay anytime this month but we are not sure if she would make good with her promise as she failed to pay on her promised dates in the past.

May we also remind you that under our lease contract, the 2 months security deposit cannot be applied against unpaid rentals and shall be released one month after the move-out.

The situation has been like this since September of last year, to the point of reaching four (4) months of rental unpaid at one time. Due to this, we are inclined not to renew the lease come March 10.

We felt we need to inform you also of the situation since you are a co-lessee together with your wife, Carol. Kindly help her settle the outstanding rent within five (5) days from this date.

Thank you.
Sincerely yours,
Hilda Burkhart
Lessor
Cell # (710) 913-3495

Directions: **Write Ms. Burkhart and acknowledge your responsibilities, but explain that you have been stationed overseas for the last year and had no idea that the rent wasn't being paid. Propose a solution.**

Questions 6-7: Respond to a written request

答題範例

Question 7

From:	Ron Swanson <r_swanson@latimes.com
To:	Hilda Burkhart <hilda@burkhartrentals.com
Re:	Unpaid Rentals for Unit 7-B Mandarin Gardens
Date:	February 13

Ms. Burkhart,

Of course, I am well aware of my responsibilities as a co-lessee; however, as you are well aware, I have been working on assignment in Saudi Arabia for the last year. During this time, I have sent my wife more than enough money to cover all living expenses, including the rent. Therefore, this news comes as a complete shock to me.

If you would kindly send me your bank information, I will promptly wire you the unpaid balance. Please accept my apologies for this unfortunate situation. I appreciate you letting me know about it.

Sincerely,
Ron Swanson

GO ON TO THE NEXT PAGE.

Questions 8: Write an opinion essay

Question 8

Directions: Read the question below. You have 30 minutes to plan, write, and revise your essay. Typically, an effective response will contain a minimum of 300 words.

Some people believe that freedom of speech is essential in a democratic society, while others believe that the right to free speech is frequently abused and must be limited for the good of society. Provide reasons or examples to support your opinion.

Questions 8: Write an opinion essay

答題範例

Question 8

The characteristics of a true democracy are the right of citizens to choose their government representatives, a government with limited powers, majority rule, minority rights, and effective checks and balances on the government. Democracies are maintained through rule of law as established by a written constitution. Democracies take one of two main forms. Direct democracies allow citizens to directly participate in making public policy, so it is more feasible for smaller communities. Representative democracies are set up so citizens vote for representatives who actually make the laws instead of voting directly on each law.

Freedom of expression and the separation of the state from social and business organizations are both essential for a democracy to function effectively. In countries where the government controls the press or operates businesses, abuses of power can undermine attempts at establishing and maintaining a democracy.

Moreover, freedom of expression is important for democracy, because it enables the public to participate in making decisions based on the free flow of information and ideas. Without it, people would be unable to make informed decisions. In 1946, the United Nations General Assembly stated that freedom of expression is a fundamental human right. The right to vote, for example, stems from freedom of expression, which allows citizens to share ideas and watch political debates and campaigns about politicians and their ideologies. Without this exchange of ideas, citizens wouldn't be informed on the issues. Freedom of expression envelops freedom of speech, freedom of religion and freedom of thought.

Although it is true that these rights can be abused, we already have laws in place that define and prosecute types of speech which do not qualify as free speech; for instance, slander, libel, and defamation. However, freedom of expression is more than just having an opinion about something. Oftentimes, governments try to censor journalists who cover sensitive issues. Human rights organizations depend on free speech. Without the ability of the people to communicate freely, the abovementioned abuses of power are inevitable. Therefore, there is no need to tighten restrictions on the flow of information.

TOEIC ANSWER SHEET

LISTENING SECTION

Part 1

No.	ANSWER A B C D
1	Ⓐ Ⓑ Ⓒ Ⓓ
2	Ⓐ Ⓑ Ⓒ Ⓓ
3	Ⓐ Ⓑ Ⓒ Ⓓ
4	Ⓐ Ⓑ Ⓒ Ⓓ
5	Ⓐ Ⓑ Ⓒ Ⓓ
6	Ⓐ Ⓑ Ⓒ Ⓓ
7	Ⓐ Ⓑ Ⓒ Ⓓ
8	Ⓐ Ⓑ Ⓒ
9	Ⓐ Ⓑ Ⓒ
10	Ⓐ Ⓑ Ⓒ

Part 2

No.	ANSWER A B C D
11	Ⓐ Ⓑ Ⓒ
12	Ⓐ Ⓑ Ⓒ
13	Ⓐ Ⓑ Ⓒ
14	Ⓐ Ⓑ Ⓒ
15	Ⓐ Ⓑ Ⓒ
16	Ⓐ Ⓑ Ⓒ
17	Ⓐ Ⓑ Ⓒ
18	Ⓐ Ⓑ Ⓒ
19	Ⓐ Ⓑ Ⓒ
20	Ⓐ Ⓑ Ⓒ
21	Ⓐ Ⓑ Ⓒ
22	Ⓐ Ⓑ Ⓒ
23	Ⓐ Ⓑ Ⓒ
24	Ⓐ Ⓑ Ⓒ
25	Ⓐ Ⓑ Ⓒ
26	Ⓐ Ⓑ Ⓒ
27	Ⓐ Ⓑ Ⓒ
28	Ⓐ Ⓑ Ⓒ
29	Ⓐ Ⓑ Ⓒ
30	Ⓐ Ⓑ Ⓒ
31	Ⓐ Ⓑ Ⓒ

Part 3

No.	ANSWER A B C D
32	Ⓐ Ⓑ Ⓒ Ⓓ
33	Ⓐ Ⓑ Ⓒ Ⓓ
34	Ⓐ Ⓑ Ⓒ Ⓓ
35	Ⓐ Ⓑ Ⓒ Ⓓ
36	Ⓐ Ⓑ Ⓒ Ⓓ
37	Ⓐ Ⓑ Ⓒ Ⓓ
38	Ⓐ Ⓑ Ⓒ Ⓓ
39	Ⓐ Ⓑ Ⓒ Ⓓ
40	Ⓐ Ⓑ Ⓒ Ⓓ
41	Ⓐ Ⓑ Ⓒ Ⓓ
42	Ⓐ Ⓑ Ⓒ Ⓓ
43	Ⓐ Ⓑ Ⓒ Ⓓ
44	Ⓐ Ⓑ Ⓒ Ⓓ
45	Ⓐ Ⓑ Ⓒ Ⓓ
46	Ⓐ Ⓑ Ⓒ Ⓓ
47	Ⓐ Ⓑ Ⓒ Ⓓ
48	Ⓐ Ⓑ Ⓒ Ⓓ
49	Ⓐ Ⓑ Ⓒ Ⓓ
50	Ⓐ Ⓑ Ⓒ Ⓓ
51–70	Ⓐ Ⓑ Ⓒ Ⓓ

Part 4

No.	ANSWER A B C D
71–100	Ⓐ Ⓑ Ⓒ Ⓓ

READING SECTION

Part 5

No.	ANSWER A B C D
101–130	Ⓐ Ⓑ Ⓒ Ⓓ

Part 6

No.	ANSWER A B C D
131–146	Ⓐ Ⓑ Ⓒ Ⓓ

Part 7

No.	ANSWER A B C D
147–200	Ⓐ Ⓑ Ⓒ Ⓓ

REGISTRATION No.

姓 名

N A M E

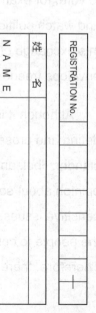